D0522196

THE
CAPTAIN
AND THE
GLORY

Also by Dave Eggers

FICTION

The Parade
Heroes of the Frontier
Your Fathers, Where Are They? And the Prophets, Do They Live Forever?
The Circle
A Hologram for the King
What Is the What
How We Are Hungry
You Shall Know Our Velocity!

MEMOIR

A Heartbreaking Work of Staggering Genius

NONFICTION

The Monk of Mokha
Understanding the Sky
Zeitoun

THE
CAPTAIN
AND THE
GLORY

an entertainment

DAVE EGGERS

HAMISH HAMILTON
an imprint of
PENGUIN BOOKS

HAMISH HAMILTON

UK | USA | Canada | Ireland | Australia
India | New Zealand | South Africa

Hamish Hamilton is part of the Penguin Random House group of companies
whose addresses can be found at global.penguinrandomhouse.com.

First published in the United States of America by Alfred A. Knopf 2019
First published in Great Britain by Hamish Hamilton 2019
001

Copyright © Dave Eggers, 2019

Illustrations by Nathaniel Russell

The moral right of the author has been asserted

This is a work of fiction. Names, characters, places and incidents either are the product
of the author's imagination or are used fictitiously. Any resemblance to nefarious public officials
responsible for the suffering of countless innocents is entirely metaphorical.

Printed and bound in Great Britain by Clays Ltd, Elcograf S.p.A.

A CIP catalogue record for this book is available from the British Library

ISBN: 978-0-241-44595-2

www.greenpenguin.co.uk

THE
CAPTAIN
AND THE
GLORY

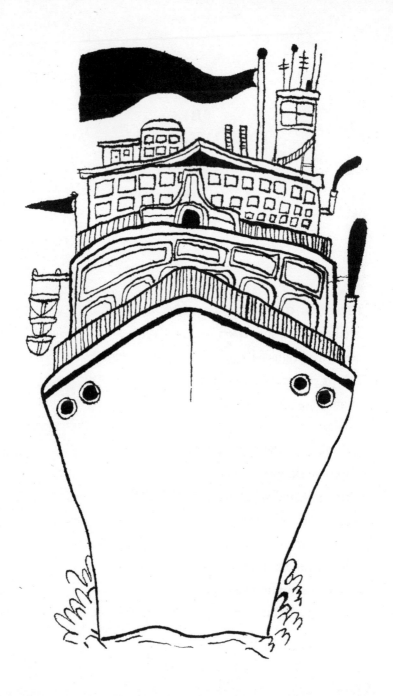

I

THE AGING CAPTAIN, gray at the temples now, had steered the great ship *Glory* for many years, and was ready to retire. On a bright fall day of white clouds and melancholy, the ship's passengers, thousands of them, gathered to see him off. They were docked at a lush tropical isle, where the departing captain planned to retire, to eat the freshest fruit and drink from the purest springs. He had been a kind and unflappable skipper for many years, through seas turbulent and tranquil, and watching him descend the gangplank brought more than a few of the *Glory*'s passengers to tears.

Among the citizens of the ship there were carpenters and teachers, painters and professors and plumbers, and they had come to the ship from the planet's every corner. They did not always agree on everything, but they shared a history,

3

and over centuries together they had faced death and birth, glorious sunrises and nights of unease, war and sorrow and triumph and tragedy. Through it all they had developed a sense that they were a mad, ragged quilt of humanity, full of color and contradiction, but unwilling to be separated or torn.

With the old captain leaving, the passengers talked about who should succeed him. It was a daunting task. The departing captain was both war hero and learned man, was indeed so accomplished a sailor and diplomat that he had earned the nickname the Admiral—an honorific never given to another captain before him.

There were a number of possible replacements for the Admiral—a dozen or so crew members who had steered great ships before, who knew nautical navigation and maritime law. There were at least ten, in fact, who had worked on this particular ship for decades and knew its every last gauge and gudgeon. As the passengers were contemplating which of these qualified persons could take the helm, one of the passengers spoke up.

"I'll do it," he said loudly with a voice at once high-pitched and hoarse. This man was large and lumpy, and a bit hunched over, and wore a yellow feather in his hair. All the passengers knew him well. They knew him to be the guy who sold cheap souvenirs near the putt-putt golf course, who had borrowed money from all of the ship's adults and some of its teenagers, who swindled rubes via three-card monte and pig-in-the-poke, who stayed inside on windy or rainy days (because the effect on his feather was catastrophic) and who said pretty much anything that popped into his head.

"I like that guy," said one passenger. "He says anything that pops into his head."

"Yeah!" yelled another. This man's nickname was Fingers, because he regularly stole passengers' wallets and purses, and specialized in stealing candy from children. Fingers was close friends with the man with the yellow feather, and the two of them were part of a coterie of petty thieves and confidence men who typically gathered under the stairs near the women's locker room so they could take upskirt photos. Among them was Ed the Unwashed, who laundered money, and Sweetie, who resold the candy Fingers had stolen from children. There was a blackmailer named Benny the Squeeze, a murderer named Patsy the Murderer, and a patsy named Michael the Cohen. There was a knee-breaker named Freddie the Whack, and a nattily dressed racketeer named Paul the Manafort, and they both—they all—led the cheers for the man with the yellow feather. They and the rest of the Upskirt Boys—for that was what they called themselves—were greatly amused by the idea of their buddy, whom they all secretly considered almost unbearably vulgar and thin-skinned and having an oniony, old-man smell, becoming captain.

"Let me be captain!" the man with the yellow feather yelled. He had never been a captain before. He had never steered a ship of any kind or size, and had insulted the previous captains loudly and often. In fact, for years this man had been telling his fellow passengers how much he didn't even like boats. He had said, over and over, that all ships were bad, and everyone running them was bad. In fact, he loathed everyone on the ship, unless they were willing to loan him money or were women-in-bathing-suits.

"Let me be captain!" he said again.

Fingers and Sweetie and Pete the Pipe—forgot to mention Pete the Pipe; he hit people with pipes—laughed, because the idea of their friend becoming captain was demented. It was bonkers. Many other passengers laughed, too, because all the passengers knew the man with the yellow feather to be clownish and not the least bit qualified. He was also known to all as someone who lied so often it was considered involuntary and incurable. When he had $43 in his pocket he said he had $76. When he lost at cards or golf, he walked away, then told the first person he encountered that he'd won. When there was no reason to lie, he lied. He lied about the time of day while standing under a clock. Between that and the fact that he often joked crudely, everyone assumed that this, too, was a lie or crude joke.

"This time I'm not lying or joking," he said, and put on a

serious face, pouting his lips as serious people do. Then he put his hand on his heart, and sang a patriotic song for as long as he could remember the words.

This patriotism was confusing to those passengers who remembered that when the ship had been at war some years ago, and all the young men and women of the *Glory* had fought with swords and cannons to protect the ship and its thousands of innocents, the man with the yellow feather had hidden in the bowels of the ship looking through pornographic magazines.

"Let's hear him out," said a grandfather of nine who in every way was sensible and true.

The passengers asked the man with the yellow feather how he felt about taxes.

"Only suckers pay them," he said.

"Hooray!" said many of the passengers. They thought this a novel approach to paying taxes—to not pay them. With that one statement, the candidacy of the man with the yellow feather gained considerable momentum.

"I declare," said the grandfather of nine who in every way was sensible and true, "that we need someone like this to shake things up."

The passengers all mulled this idea, and began discussing it in earnest. The idea of shaking things up—anything from one's toothpaste to one's shoes—held a certain inherent appeal to most of the ship's citizens. To them, shaking things up held the promise, however irrational and unproven, that everything shaken, or tossed randomly into the air, might come down better. Somehow, in the flying and falling, steel might become gold, sadness might become triumph, what had been good might become great.

"Shake things up! Shake things up!" This chant was started by a gaggle of teenage boys, who were only half-serious, and who had most recently been seen urinating their names onto the shuffleboard court.

Amid the noise, the ship's first mate, a courageous woman who had stood by the previous captain's side for too many years to count, stepped forward.

"My fellow passengers," she said, "with all due respect, the last thing we need is someone shaking things up. This is a ship. A ship full of humans, all of them in our care. Outside, the ocean is vast and deep and teeming with the unknown— from squalls to sharks to typhoons. The sea provides enough uncertainty and chaos. The last thing we need is a captain providing *more* of all that."

But many passengers had become intrigued with the notion of the man with the yellow feather occupying the most important position on the ship. There had long been a maxim on the ship, uttered by every parent to every child, that stated, "On this ship, anyone can grow up to be captain."

It was a dictum that spoke of the ship's dedication to opportunity and equality and an ostensibly classless society. When this maxim was first expressed, though, its originator meant that from any humble beginning, through decades of rigorous study and apprenticeship, through certifications and examinations, anyone might eventually ascend to the captain's chair.

But over the years, this notion had come to mean that any imbecile might decide on a certain Monday to become a captain, and by Tuesday, with no qualifications whatsoever, that imbecile could take charge of a 300,000-ton vessel and the thousands of lives contained within.

To underline the point, one thoughtful man stepped forward, a pedagogical index finger in the air. "If we truly believe that anyone can grow up to be captain," he said, "we should prove it by electing the least qualified, least respected person on the ship—a man who has never done anything for anyone but himself, a man who has palpable disdain for all previous captains, and no respect at all for the builders of the ship, its history, or anything it stands for."

To many of the passengers, this made a wonderful kind of sense. To prove they were all equal, they should, the logic followed, be led by a known moron.

Amid the discussion, a girl of twelve stepped forward. Her name was Ava. As a child, Ava did not have a say in the voting over who would guide the vessel, but still she spoke up. "I've been listening to this debate," she said, "and I have to say I'm flabbergasted that this idea is even being entertained. There's no way a rational group of adults would ever give such power to a man like this, over our very lives— a man who has absolutely no relevant experience, who has never sailed even a dinghy—a man known only for a crude mouth and a yellow feather, a man who at this very moment is trying to feel up my mother"—for he was feeling up the girl's mother just then.

"Give yourselves some credit," Ava said. "We are a noble people with a storied history. We deserve to be led by the most enlightened, reasonable and honorable among us, not the loudest, cruelest, most selfish and most foul."

II

"I LIKE BEING CAPTAIN," said the man with the yellow feather. He was installed high on the bridge of the *Glory,* and surveyed the seas with swelling pride. The ship's passengers had elected him to steer the ship and he was very pleased about it.

The supporters of the new Captain were pleased, too. In fact, they were jubilant. Never in their lifetimes had something like this happened. They felt triumphant and unstoppable and capable of anything. To celebrate the unprecedented victory, they planned a parade to honor the new Captain, to be held later that day. While some supporters were festooning the ship with bunting and balloons, a group of the Captain's most ardent fans—too excited to be effective decorators— instead found a pair of passengers who had supported the

11

previous captain, and they beat them with clubs and hammers, thinking joyfully of the new Captain with every blow. While they beat their opposition, they got word that the Admiral had just died. So shocked and disappointed was he in the ascendance of the *Glory*'s worst passenger, that his head froze and his heart burst simultaneously, causing the rest of his body to give up, too. This news, though sad for many, was very satisfying to the most fervent supporters of the man with the yellow feather. It made them feel not just triumphant but liberated, too—free from history, free from all that was staid and stuffy and stale.

And yet there was something that nagged at these supporters of the man with the yellow feather. When the little girl had given her speech, in which she called the new Captain, and by inference his supporters, "most foul," it had stung. In fact it really hurt.

But then a few of the Captain's most besotted supporters had an idea. And the idea was to own it. In preparation for the parade, they attached to their clothing thousands of chicken feathers and fashioned beaks from paper plates. On their chests they wrote the words MOST FOUL and they strutted around the ship, much to the delight of the Captain's other supporters. The Upskirt Boys considered them daffy and grotesque, but they said nothing, hoping the feathered nonsense would catch on.

12

It did. In short order, dozens more supporters created their own Most Foul costumes, some of them using the aviary spelling of the word, each of them choosing to dress as whatever bird reflected their personality. And thus, when the parade began, and the Captain was carried on a litter through the  crowds, he saw his supporters costumed as hens and roosters, roadrunners and condors, chickadees and cockatoos. They held signs that read, A CAPTAIN MOST FOUL! and they cheered the new captain with abandon. When the Captain came near, they tried to touch him but he recoiled, because he considered them filthy simpletons who carried unnameable and uncountable contagions and germs.

Otherwise, though, it was a wonderful parade, and the new Captain wished it could have lasted forever. The idea of standing on the bridge, navigating and steering all day, held less appeal than being cheered by people dressed in handmade avian costumes. At the end of the parade, he was carried to the bridge, where he met the eyes of a dozen crew members there to assist him, none of whom he trusted. He looked at all the screens and levers and buttons, and he whistled. "There sure are a lot of screens and buttons here!"

He whistled again. "This is already more complicated than I thought," he thought.

He decided he needed some help. Immediately his mind turned to a woman he'd been seeing around the ship. He'd been watching her for as long as he could remember, admiring her comely heart-shaped face and her glorious figure and her hair, which was silky and straight and as yellow as his feather. He often talked to other men about how attractive she was, and how good she smelled, and how much he'd like to date her. He wanted such a gorgeous creature near him always, so he asked her if she would help him steer the ship.

"Okay, Dad," she said.

III

WITH HIS DAUGHTER by his side, the Captain felt much better. His daughter had brought her doll, though, and the sight of it, a limp boy-doll with rosy cheeks and black, vacant eyes, always gave him pause. There was something at once vacuous and sinister about the lifeless faux-boy, but his daughter loved that doll, so the Captain had no choice but to accept the two of them as a package. There were other elements around him, though, that the Captain found more irritating.

"Who are all these people around us?" he asked.

"That's the crew, Dad. They help steer the ship. That's the chief engineer, and that's the staff captain, and that's the—"

"Stop," the Captain said, "please stop," his brain already hurting from all the terminology. The Captain felt uneasy around people he had not hired himself, and to make matters worse, many of the crew members on the bridge had mustaches, and the Captain felt uneasy around mustaches. The Captain floated the idea to his daughter of firing all of the men and women on the bridge, and the Captain's daughter shrugged. She did not consider firing the entire navigational staff a good idea, but then again, she did not believe, as the Captain's main adviser, that it was her place to tell him.

The Captain pictured himself telling all these people that they were dismissed, or fired. He had a wonderful vision of himself standing straight in front of them and saying, "You're all relieved of your duties! You have one minute to vacate the bridge!" In his vision he was very tall and strong, and the staff was very meek and intimidated.

But the idea of actually firing anyone gave him a stomachache, so he asked his daughter to do it. Shrugging, she dismissed the staff captain, the chief engineer, the quartermaster, the chief radio operator, the safety officers, the starbolins, on and on—in short, everyone on the ship who knew how to operate the ship and was within earshot.

When they were gone, the bridge was empty and the Captain felt much more at ease. For a few minutes, the Captain and his daughter and her doll sat in silence, each of them already bored and each of them wishing they could be somewhere else.

"I'm gonna make an announcement," the Captain said.

"Sounds good, Dad," his daughter said.

He turned on the microphone that broadcast to the entire ship. "We will take you on a voyage you will never forget!" he said.

That was a good start, he thought, and his daughter, and many of the passengers, agreed.

"So where should we go?" the daughter asked her father.

The Captain brightened. "I want to go somewhere really tremendous," he said. "Somewhere that's better than anywhere we've been before, but also like the past, and also yellow." The Captain, his daughter, and her doll stood for a while on the bridge, thinking of where someplace like that might be.

Night came on, and no thoughts had come to any one of them. For a moment, sometime after midnight, the doll's vacant eyes seemed to flicker briefly, but it was simply a trick of the light.

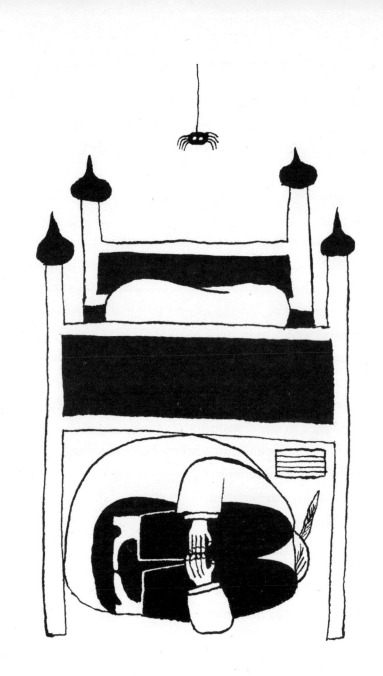

IV

FOR AS LONG as he could remember, the man with the yellow feather had trouble sleeping. His head was full of arguments and recriminations, and in the dark he turned in his bed like a restless kitten.

When he was chosen to steer the ship, he held out the vague hope that his new quarters and new position might bring with them better rest, but this was not to be. The first night in his stateroom bed, he couldn't sleep at all.

The Captain was lying prone, staring at the ceiling as he usually did, waiting for sleep but instead fighting a thousand battles in his mind against his former teachers who had not thought him brilliant, all the women who did not swoon when he pushed his genitals at them in elevators and on streets, and all the passengers on the boat who had not voted to make him captain.

Then came the spider. It was simply there, on the ceiling, upside down, as if it had been there all along, somehow defying gravity—defying the sanctity and cleanliness of his stateroom. It scampered determinedly across the ceiling and then stopped directly over his bed. Directly over his face! The Captain muffled a scream. Then, slowly, so as not to invite the possibility of the spider noticing him and descending upon him, the Captain inched his way off the bed and, with a thump much too loud for his subterfuge, fell onto the floor and rolled himself into the corner.

He looked up. No! The spider had followed him on the ceiling, as if mirroring his movements. The Captain let out a whimper, for he was afraid often, hourly in fact, of everything from germs to women-not-wearing-bathing-suits to jai alai, but he was certain he'd never been so afraid as when he looked up and saw that spider on the ceiling over him.

The Captain knew he could not get back into that bed. Perhaps not ever. He also knew that he was not safe anywhere in the stateroom. But then he had an idea. From his vantage point he could see that the bed was higher than the average bed, and had quite a bit of clearance underneath the mattress. If he could scamper from the corner of the room and slither under the bed, he could stay there, perhaps even sleep there, knowing that the spider could not see him and could not get at him.

And so the Captain moved in a serpentine way from his corner of the room to the space under the bed, feeling sure at any moment the spider would descend upon him, would touch him with its tiny serrated limbs . . . But then the Captain made it. When he arrived in the claustrophobic darkness under the bed, he felt immeasurable relief. He was safe there, unseen there, and knew instantly that this was where he would sleep that night and all nights thereafter—on the floor, under his bed.

"Psst," said a voice. The Captain looked left and right, worrying briefly that the spider tormenting him was the kind of spider that could talk.

"Psst," the voice said again. Now the Captain located the source of the sound. It was coming from the vent on the wall next to the bed. He inched closer to it.

"Yes?" he said into the vent.

"Captain," the voice said, distant but insistent. "I have much to tell you. First, I must congratulate you on eluding and outsmarting that terrifying arachnid. Spiders, as a man of your intellect no doubt knows, are the world's most dangerous carriers of germs, and also they cause rectal bleeding."

The Captain did not know these spider-facts involving germs and rectal bleeding, but he did not let the voice in the

21

vent know he did not know these things. He liked the sound of the word *intellect* being applied to him, and did not want to risk its new proximity to his name.

"This ship has long had a problem with spiders, as you of course are aware," the voice in the vent said. "We are practically in*fest*ed with them. It's a big problem, a disgrace really, and could lead to the destruction of the ship and maybe the world."

The Captain had never seen a spider on this ship, and had never heard anyone speak of a spider on this ship—which is why the sight of the one on his ceiling had given him such terror. But now that the voice in the vent mentioned it, the Captain was certain that he had in fact heard about the spider problem, that it was a big problem, a disgrace really, was in fact an infestation that threatened the ship and the world.

"I, too, have made the rational choice to sleep under the bed," the voice in the vent said. "It keeps me safe from the rectal-bleeding spiders, and also certain people who make me uncomfortable, like for instance anyone who might be called swarthy."

The Captain felt a great smile overtake his face. This voice coming from the vent, more than anyone he'd ever met—even his daughter, who was a solid 9—understood him. The Captain, too, was made uncomfortable by certain people who might be called swarthy, but had never thought

22

that simply hiding under his bed would be the solution. But it was!

And so, because the Captain was awake, and had nothing else to do, he listened closely over the next few hours, as the voice in the vent said a great many fascinating things, so many things that the Captain had suspected but had never felt the courage to say. The voice in the vent advanced a quite rational theory that it was actually 297 years earlier than commonly believed, and this was the fault of Pope Sylvester (a very bad guy). He explained that certain sandwiches were not good. He explained that the historic adversaries of the *Glory*—various pirate crews who plagued the seas, looting and beheading innocents—were in fact admirable go-getters that the Captain would be wise to work with on various initiatives. He lucidly explained that the crew members who worked in the engine room were plotting against the Captain, and he said that the ship would be better if certain people, who looked a certain way and were from certain places, were to be thrown overboard.

The Captain listened, rapt, as the voice in the vent went on, listing the many things there were to fear and hate and the various ways the world not-under-the-bed was terrifying and perilous. The Captain felt at last that someone was expressing his innermost thoughts. Like the voice in the vent, the Captain loathed most people and suspected that beneath

23

every seeming-simple truth there was a sinister lie. Like the voice in the vent, the Captain was angry and bewildered by so many things: salad, for starters, and also dictionaries, and ranch houses, and mustaches of course, and women-not-wearing-bathing-suits. The voice in the vent was angry and bewildered by all these things, too, and had very brilliant theories about these fearful factors, how they were connected in a coordinated way designed to undermine the Captain and make the ship less good. As the voice in the vent continued, the Captain felt himself growing stronger. He felt, as the voice talked through the night, that he had made a true friend, an advocate, an ally—a north star.

V

WHEN THE SHIP'S passengers woke that morning and went to breakfast, the cafeteria wipe-away board, which customarily described the day's weather and menu, now featured a series of messages scrawled in the handwriting of a child.

RECTAL BLEEDING SPIDERS RUNNING AMOK ON SHIP :(

*

PEOPLE WHO "RUN" ENGINES ARE YOUR ENEMIES.

*

MY P-NUS: WOMEN HAVE ENJOYED!!

*

ALSO PROBABLY SOME PEOPLE WILL BE
THROWN OVERBORED SOON.

As the passengers ate their breakfast, they puzzled over the messages on the board. They knew they were written by the Captain, for the Captain's crude handwriting was distinctive, and he was the only adult on the ship inclined to misspell common words, capitalize at random, and use frowny-faces at the ends of sentences.

The passengers deduced that the Captain had woken up before anyone else, and had come down to the cafeteria to write messages, entirely unrelated to the work of steering the ship, on a wipe-away board that usually contained notices about rain and soup.

"This is quite different than before," one of the passengers said. And no one could argue the point. Things had changed.

After breakfast, the business and leisure of the ship's passengers went on more or less as before. Children played ping-pong and puttered in the pool and parents watched and worried and strolled the promenades. There was work done in offices and gardens and galleries and libraries. There were parties, picnics, and potlucks, though during all of these everyday activities, the passengers were faintly distracted by the thought of the Captain's septuagenarian phallus and the women against whom he might have rubbed it. And, they thought, didn't he also mention something about people being thrown overboard? There were hundreds of discussions throughout the day about the new Captain and his new way of communicating.

"I find it refreshing," one woman said. "He speaks his mind."

"He writes like I speak when I'm drunk," another man said, "and I find that comforting."

For as long as the passengers could remember, every previous captain had simply been the Captain, distinguished and calm, guiding the ship and occasionally appearing at dinner in formal attire. When these previous captains spoke at all, they had expressed themselves with quiet reserve and dignity. They used complicated words regularly, and while giving speeches, they read from note cards—all of which, the supporters of the new captain realized, conveyed dishonesty and a certain palpable elitism.

In the eyes of the Most Foul, though, this new captain was candid and unvarnished. And because he didn't know how to spell, and had no taste or manners or filter or shame or sense of what was true and what was false—because he was unscripted when he told lies—he was the most honest captain they'd ever known.

That first morning, when they saw his scrawlings on the wipe-away board, these passengers realized that all along, what they had wanted from their captain were not bland messages about the weather and food. What they wanted all along were garbled messages, written before dawn, about the captain's fears, enemies, and penis.

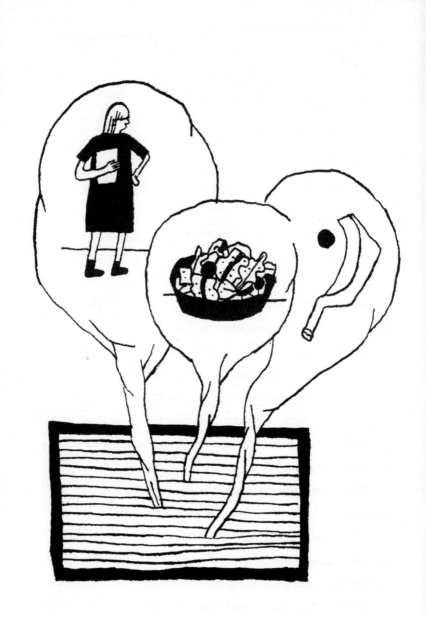

VI

FOR THE CAPTAIN, putting his most personal and
troubled thoughts onto a wipe-away board for all to see
relieved a volcanic pressure within him. On the morning
of his first wipe-away messages, almost immediately after
rendering his last misspelled word, his solace was profound.
He scampered back to the bridge and his mind was so restful
and unburdened that he lay down on his bed—under his
bed—to take a nap.

"Psst," the voice said. "Nice going with the messages on
the board."

The Captain's heart swelled. Though he'd only known
the voice in the vent for a short time, he felt that next to his
beautiful daughter—who had been wearing a really sexy
number that day, angora probably, he couldn't get it out of his

mind, good god—there was no one whose approval he sought and valued more.

The Captain and the voice in the vent had another wonderful talk that night. The voice in the vent told him about how clouds were full of chemicals that reduced sperm count, and that most forks were covered in pubic hair and should not be used. He explained that pork was actually putty and that all books were written by people who could not get erections and who were plotting against the Captain, in league with the spiders-with-rectal-bleeding. He also reminded the Captain that it was high time he threw some people overboard.

The next morning, the passengers on the ship read a new series of messages on the wipe-away board.

ALSO ABOUT MY P-NUS: MUCH BETTER
THAN PREVIOUS CAPTAIN'S.

*

THIS WEEK: EVERYONE GETS AN XTRA $1.50!

*

SOME PASSENGERS TO BE THROWN IN OCEAN SOON!!

*

HAPPY SINCO DE MAYO

The ship's passengers, even the Most Foul, were conflicted. They were pleased that they would be receiving another $1.50 that week, but they were also concerned about the spiders who caused bleeding, and the fact that the Captain had been captain for many days, and the ship had not yet left port.

VII

THAT MORNING, HIGH ABOVE, the Captain stood on the bridge, looking around him. As he scanned the horizon, he noticed something. The ship did not seem to be moving. He turned to his daughter. "Why are we not moving?" he asked her.

"There are no people currently navigating the ship," she said. "Remember when we fired everyone?"

The Captain looked at her and knew she was right. She was always right. She was so smart, he thought. She was also so gorgeous, and curvaceous, and so demure that when he thought of her, his mind went caterwauling into unsavory places.

"We do have this," she said, and retrieved a very thick book, its cover bright orange, that read *Ship's Manual* on its spine. His daughter began paging through it, oohing and even ahhing, noting the level of detail and instruction contained within and making sounds of gratitude and relief.

"Can I see that?" he said, and snatched the book from his daughter's beautiful hands. He left the bridge and walked to the railing and threw the book overboard. Its pages briefly fanned, like a bird in spastic flight, before its covers closed again and the book hit the sea with a stentorian slap. The Captain watched the manual sink quickly in the violet sea.

But it did not, in fact, sink. It continued to float on the water. "Why isn't that thing sinking?" the Captain asked.

"I don't know, Dad," his daughter said. "It's probably designed to float."

The Captain watched as the book got smaller as the tide took it away from the *Glory,* and though he would have preferred it to sink without a trace, at least it was gone, and the tightening in his chest that he'd felt in its presence was gone, too. Books like that, he felt, were for people without natural talent and without innate leadership ability, and worse, they implied that there had been captains before the Captain and that there would be captains after, and both notions made the Captain feel something approaching insignificance, and this was a kind of affront against the Captain that he could not abide. He felt sure he needed a cheeseburger made by teenagers and wrapped in paper.

After eating his cheeseburger made by teenagers and wrapped in paper, the Captain and his daughter and her doll then went about filling the roles of all the crew members they had fired. But because the Captain was suspicious of anyone who had done a job before, he chose carefully, to ensure that no one he hired to handle any part of the ship had ever seen that part of the ship before.

In the role of chief engineer, he put a man he'd met by the pool one day and who said he liked the captain's feather. In the role of first officer, he placed one of his daughter's friends, who had long legs and gorgeous hair and had many times allowed the Captain to stare at her while she ate salad. In the role of chief electrician, he put Eddie the Whack. In the place of chief navigator, he put Pete the Pipe. In fact, he found spots for all of his old friends. Fingers handled the money, Sweetie handled the food, Patsy the Murderer took over the infirmary, and Paul the Manafort oversaw the ship's office of ethics and accountability. The ship's pet shelter was replaced by an abattoir. The ship's teachers were replaced by cops. The ship's theater group was replaced by a television. The ship's librarian was replaced by a television. The ship's historian was replaced by a television. The ship's symphony was replaced by a television playing patriotic songs, and to head up the agency that supported small businesses, the Captain appointed the wife of the guy who ran the World Wrestling Federation.

The one group of people he was not allowed to replace—it was an unbreakable rule of the ship, and thus he considered it a disgrace—were those in the engine room. Because the voice in the vent had instructed him not to talk to the engine-room people (because they were his enemies) the Captain told his daughter to tell Fingers to call the engine room and have them start the engines. It worked. They started the engines, and the boat groaned awake.

"Now what?" he asked his daughter.

Together they looked at the controls. The Captain hoped he might find a button that said FORWARD or STRAIGHT, but there was no such button.

"I think I've got it," his daughter said. The Captain turned to find her reading a book; immediately his stomach tightened. "I think you can just hold the wheel straight," she said, "and it will go straight."

The Captain put his hands on the wheel and found that without moving it at all, the ship slowly and majestically left port and sailed into the open sea. It was clear to him, at that moment, that he was the greatest captain that had ever captained.

VIII

AFTER A FEW MINUTES, though, the Captain grew bored.

Standing alone on the bridge was boring. And the sea ahead was boring. It didn't move! The horizon was just the horizon, and the sun was just the sun, and there weren't even any clouds or storms to look at. Where were the whales? He saw no whales.

Then he had an idea. He nudged the wheel a bit left, and the entire ship listed leftward, which was both frightening and thrilling. He turned the wheel to the right, and the totality of the ship, and its uncountable passengers and their possessions, all were sent rightward. In the cafeteria, where the passengers were eating lunch, a thousand plates and glasses shattered. An elderly man was thrown from his chair, struck his head on the dessert cart and died later that night.

High above, the Captain was elated by the riveting drama caused by the surprises of his steering. For the first time he felt the power of the enormous ship, and felt that he'd arrived at how to make an otherwise sterile experience—that of standing more or less alone on the sealed and secure bridge of a ship—feel viscerally alive. He was so filled with energy and inspiration that he decided to deface the photographs of all the *Glory*'s previous captains.

The back wall of the bridge featured a gallery of dignified photos of all the Captain's predecessors, and ever since he'd taken the wheel, the Captain had found these portraits aggravating, given that there were so many of them, and none were of himself. So he took his wipe-away marker and drew horns and warts and missing teeth onto the other captains, starting with the captains who had built the ship, all of whom were dead and few of whom had voted for him. In fact, he realized, because they were all dead, *none* of the previous captains had voted for him, which provoked a billowing rage within the Captain which he channeled into more creative defacements of their portraits. He worked his way from the very first captains to the most recent, and when he got to a particular portrait, he stopped.

This face, that of the captain known as the Admiral, caused him great consternation. The Admiral was considered by all to be a hero of war and a paragon of dedication to the

Glory, and so many other insufferable bullshit things that got under the Captain's skin and always had.

It started during the terrible battle that the Captain had avoided by hiding in the bowels of the ship reading pornography. During that war, the Admiral—then a young man, just a midshipman—had fought bravely, and had been captured and tortured by a terrible pirate known as the Pale One. When the war with the Pale One ended, and the Admiral was returned, the passengers of the *Glory* all praised him, saying he was honorable and courageous, and every time they said these things, the Captain felt rolling waves of envy and hatred, because it seemed so unjust, that simply because someone fought bravely in a war, and was captured and tortured for years on end without giving up any information or selling out fellow sailors, why should you be called a hero? And hadn't the Captain been brave, too, when he was hiding in the ship's bowels reading pornography? He could have been caught! He could have been tried for desertion and cowardice! And yet he continued to courageously hide while regularly masturbating to naked women on glossy paper.

The Captain took not just a wipe-away marker but a permanent marker, a thick and smelly one, and drew all over the portrait of the Admiral. He drew crooked teeth, and unflattering scars, and a double chin, then a triple chin, and when he was done, he felt so good about all he'd accomplished that day that he went down to the wipe-away board and wrote the first things that came to mind.

CHEESEBURGERS ARE THE GREATEST!

*

ABOUT HALF OF PEOPLE ON SHIP = MOTHERFUCKERS

*

IF YOU DIDN'T VOTE FOR ME, MAYBE YOU WILL BE KILLED?

*

AND LET'S HEAR IT FOR THE FIREFIGHTERS. THEY
ARE THE REAL HEROS. ALSO I AM A FIREFIGHTER.

Still surging with manic energy, the Captain scampered back to the bridge and asked his daughter to arrange a party for himself. Everyone on the ship would be invited, so long as they were dressed as chickens and carried signs that praised him. His daughter arranged the event, which was held in the former library, which had been liberated from the burden of its books and could now hold far more people wearing bird costumes.

Hundreds of the Most Foul attended, and the Captain stood before his acolytes, saying the sorts of things that he'd been writing on the wipe-away board. He talked about his penis for a time, and about the relative flaccidness of the dead captains before him. He told the crowd more about the enemies in the engine room, and the spiders-with-rectal-bleeding, and then posited that all medicine caused impotence or autism—and thus, he noted, all clinics on board would soon be closed. And then, in an unscripted inspiration, he announced that from then on, starboard would be port, and port would be starboard, and all overnight people besides him would be considered enemies of the ship. The crowd cheered, because this was evidence of the shaking up of things, with the overweight members of the Most Foul chorus cheering only slightly less enthusiastically.

In the second and third hours of the rally, the Captain complained about people who had hurt his feelings by not praising him as a child and those who had hurt his feelings by not praising him in the last few days, and cursed the Admiral, who hurt his feelings most of all, by being dead and by not praising him and by implying, through his own acts of courage, that the Captain was not brave. In another spur-of-the-moment inspiration, he told the Most Foul to urinate on any photos of the Admiral that they came across. The Most Foul had for decades considered the Admiral a good man and a veritable mountain of integrity, but now that the Captain brought it up, they, too, liked the idea of urinating on the face of that uppity blowhard with all his good deeds and medals. The Admiral read books and told the truth and was monogamous and had empathetic children and all of that

41

made him so superior and smug that, come to think of it, the Most Foul had always hated him and all the lofty elitist ideals he stood for.

So they all urinated on the Admiral's photos and urinated on each other, too, because, while watching them urinate on photos of the Admiral, the Captain thought it would be funny to see all the chicken-people piss on themselves. So they did, and when they were covered with rotting feathers and the urine of their neighbors, the Most Foul felt that things were really happening and really looking up. The Captain told them to cluck and they clucked. When they didn't cluck loudly enough, he told them to fuck themselves, and they did their best to fuck themselves. Sometimes they laughed with him and sometimes they laughed at him, and in general they had the greatest of times, watching a lunatic speak his mind without filter. They chuckled to themselves, greatly satisfied that their votes had put the most ridiculous person they knew in the most powerful position on the ship, and they secretly hoped he would not somehow kill them all.

Later, under his bed, the Captain settled in for the night, feeling very satisfied, though exhausted by all the praise and clapping he'd enjoyed. His eyes were tired from all the women he'd undressed with his eyes, his muscles sore from turning the steering wheel left and right all day, maiming dozens and ending the lives of three adults and one child.

"Psst," the voice in the vent said. Hearing the voice, the Captain's heart swelled and his mind got ready to take in stimulating new ideas.

"You've been forgetful," the voice said.

The Captain's blood went cold. The voice sounded angry. The Captain valued the voice in the vent so much, and could not imagine his nights without the distant voice that helped him sleep by telling him about the myriad threats beyond his bed.

"What did you forget?" the voice asked.

The Captain was never good at quizzes. "Can I get a hint?" he asked, hoping very much that the voice would simply tell him what he'd forgotten.

"It involves Certain People?" the voice said.

The Captain thought very hard, and pursed his lips in his thinking pose, but the answer did not come.

"It involves railings?" the voice said.

The Captain was silent, and hungry, wanting very much a cheeseburger made by teenagers and wrapped in paper.

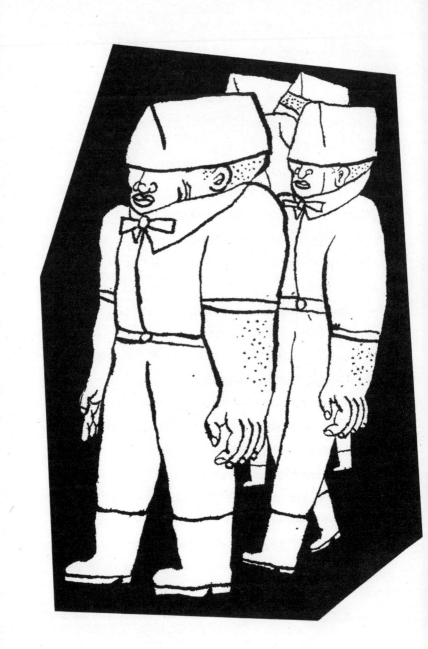

IX

FOR AS LONG as anyone could remember, new passengers
had been welcomed onto the ship, partly out of goodwill and
partly out of necessity. The ship's inhabitants were generally
generous people, so they were happy to lift from the frothing
sea those who had been storm-tossed and starving and fleeing
piracy and deprivation. It was a foundational element of all
of the faiths represented on board, each of which honored the
stranger and emphasized compassion for the most vulnerable.
And so this welcoming of the oppressed was elemental to who
the passengers believed they were: a ship of compassion and
opportunity, with the opportunity part working both ways.
The ship made itself open to these new passengers because
these new passengers were willing to take the jobs no one
else wanted, and to work three times harder than anyone else

would or could. The new passengers, happy to be safe and among new friends, and able to earn their keep, emptied the bilge and watered the plants and made the beds and cooked the food and swabbed the decks and cleaned the dishes and did a thousand things that were both invisible and essential to all. Separately but relatedly, because people sometimes died on the ship, the ship needed to replenish its population and keep the entire enterprise vital and functional. They needed new blood. And thus the system had worked since the ship had first been built, a long time ago: new people came, they were welcomed and enriched the multifaceted culture, and they helped make sure that the ship was always growing and thriving and propagating.

"*An*yway," the voice in the vent said. "No one of value is from anywhere else, or has ever been from anywhere else. The ship's most essential passengers are you and your daughter and your daughter's doll, and also cops and soldiers, and pornographic models, and your lawyers. That's pretty much it, and everyone else can go fuck themselves."

"I knew it!" the Captain said.

"Besides," the voice said, "the ship has no more room for anyone new. We're full."

Like so much of what the voice in the vent said, this information made perfect sense to the Captain, locking into logical place so many disparate and loose ideas that had long

46

rattled around the Captain's skull. Interestingly, when it came to that last part, the part about the ship being full, the voice contradicted what the Captain had seen with his own eyes. That very day, on his way to and from the rally, the Captain had seen hundreds of empty rooms, and just the other day, on some piece of paper some person gave him, he saw numbers that confirmed this, that the *Glory* had hundreds of empty rooms and many unfilled jobs. So it was not factually true that the ship was full up.

Then again, the Captain realized, the ship *could* be full up, because nothing that seemed true was ever really true, given that all truths were elitist lies perpetuated by those who did not like the Captain. And there was something about the voice in the vent, squeaky-sounding and unseen and full of suspicion and grievance, that was inherently more reliable than any document handed to the Captain, or the Captain's own eyes.

The next morning, the passengers gathered in the cafeteria for breakfast. They first read and digested the Captain's latest messages on the wipe-away board:

CHECKED ON P-NUS LAST NIGHT: STILL EXEMPLARY.

*

SPIDERS WITH BLEEDING OF RECTIM: STILL VERY BAD!

*

I "HEAR" SWIMMING POOL IS TAINTED
WITH ACID AND EBOLA

*

OTHERWISE EVERYTHING BETTER NOW—YOUR WELCOME!!

The passengers had become inured to whatever the Captain wrote on the board, and gave these messages as much thought as they gave a passing cloud. What they were thinking about was breakfast. It was Tuesday, and on Tuesday the chef usually surprised the passengers with some new dish. This morning, the chef concocted a new kind of omelet, with eggs and lamb and vegetables and cumin, and its rich smell filled the room and comforted the passengers, who were still a bit shaken from the rough sailing of the previous day.

As they were finishing their omelets and sipping coffee and tea, feeling at peace and grateful they had such a talented chef, the doors to the kitchen burst open. Two of the ship's security guards, dressed in white, pushed the cook roughly through the halls and to the stern of the boat. "What did I do?" the cook asked. "Where are we going?"

The passengers knew the men in white. They had always been part of the ship's orderly functioning, tasked with making sure that lost purses were returned, deck chairs were folded, and that drunk or disorderly passengers were brought back to their rooms to sleep. These men, because they wore white and were considered harmless and even cheerful, had been nicknamed the Snowmen.

But the passengers never before had seen the Snowmen do something like this: grab a fellow passenger at his place of work, parade him through the ship and to the outer railing. Which is what they had just done.

The passengers hurried to the deck to find the Snowmen holding the cook over the side of the ship. To the passengers it was confusing: this man had just finished preparing a delicious breakfast, and now he was dangling by his ankles over the abyss. The cook's wife and three children ran to the Snowmen, throwing themselves upon them, begging them not to let go of their husband and father. The Snowmen paid no heed and tossed the cook, whose name was Angel, overboard.

The passengers leaned over the railing and watched Angel struggle in the white swirling wake of the giant ship. His head bobbed above the surface for a time, appearing and disappearing before the seawater filled his lungs, he lost consciousness and ceased to struggle. He sank to the bottom of the sea as his wife wailed and his children, now fatherless, screamed in limitless agony.

As the ship moved on, cutting a wide path through the obsidian sea, a few passengers cheered, but most did nothing at all.

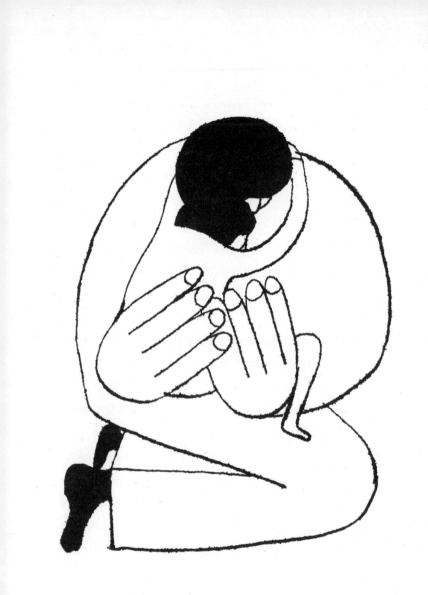

X

THE CAPTAIN SAT in his stateroom that night, watching television and eating a cheeseburger. He liked nothing better than to sit under the bed, eating cheeseburgers and watching the television he'd arranged on the floor, tilted just so, to facilitate convenient viewing.

As the Captain watched television, he saw a news report about what had happened that day when the Snowmen had thrown the cook overboard. The Captain was unsure how he felt about it. He thought the Snowmen in their clean white uniforms looked very powerful as they heaved the man overboard, and he liked that. The cook had made a big splash in the ocean when he'd plunged into it, and the Captain liked that, too. He liked how the event caused a few of the passengers to cheer.

But then he saw the mother and children wailing inconsolably, and he wasn't sure how he felt about that part. He held his cheeseburger in his hand and examined his feelings, but couldn't find the word for them.

"Psst!" a voice said. It was the voice in the vent.

The Captain was delighted to hear from the voice in the vent, for it took his mind off the confusing images he had just seen on television. The Captain put his ear to the vent and listened closely as he finished his cheeseburger.

In the morning, the Captain woke up, feeling very much refreshed, and very grateful to the voice in the vent, who had clarified so many things the night before.

First, the voice had explained that the discomfort the Captain felt about the wailing wife and children could be easily rectified by having them, too, thrown overboard. So the Captain immediately called the Snowmen and had the wife and kids woken up in the middle of the night and thrown into the ship's wake and drowned. Knowing that he would never have to hear their screaming again gave the Captain great solace and helped him sleep.

Second, the voice in the vent had explained that the Snowmen should continue throwing Certain People overboard, one or two a day, for this would instill in the passengers a sense that things were still being shaken up, that things were getting done. Throwing Certain People into the sea, the Captain readily agreed, was getting something done.

Last, the voice in the vent warned the Captain of the grave danger of those sympathetic to the cook and the cook's family becoming angry with the Captain. Thus, strengthening the security around the bridge was imperative. This would have the added benefit, the voice in the vent had noted, of keeping out the snakes with esophageal cancer—highly communicable—which had replaced the spiders-with-rectal-bleeding as the most significant animal-disease combination on board the *Glory*.

So in the morning, the Captain directed workmen to fortify the bridge with bulletproof glass and the sorts of doors and locks used in the ship's brig. At the end of the day, the workmen were finished and had done a fine job. But in their appearance and odor—for they were swarthy men and had spent the day laboring—they reminded the Captain too much of the cook and other Certain People, so he called the Snowmen and had the workers thrown overboard, too.

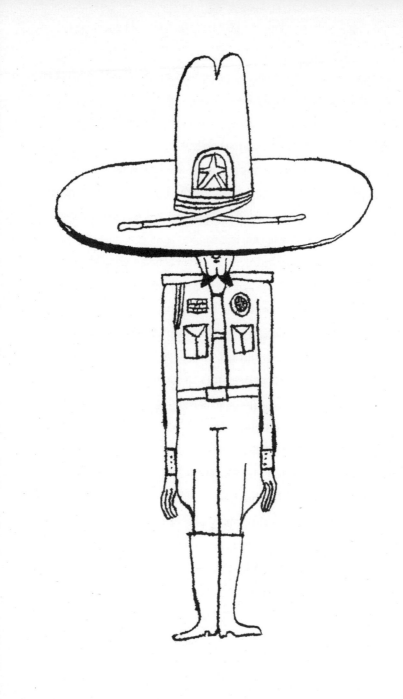

XI

LIFE ON THE SHIP settled into a kind of routine. In the morning, passengers would read the Captain's messages about spiders, his penis, and the enemies in the engine room, and afterward, the passengers would try to get on with the business of their day. Sometime around lunch, the Captain would grow bored and would steer the ship hard left and hard right, sending all objects and people not battened down careening through the ship, bones and glass shattering against walls and floors. Sometimes he would make announcements over the intercom, warning that he might start a war with another ship, and then, a few hours later, tell all the passengers on the *Glory* that he had changed his mind, or had been joking, or had never said anything like that in the first place.

In the afternoons and evenings, the Snowmen would hunt

the day's quarry. Usually there was a loud and violent struggle as they brought their victims to the rail, but always the result was the same: the Certain Person would be tossed over the side and into the churning sea. These were mothers, fathers, teachers, nurses, carpenters, bartenders, florists, maids, scientists, and cooks. Those victims would briefly struggle before their lungs filled with seawater, whereupon they would suffocate, lose consciousness and sink to the bottom of the ocean.

Sometime after dinner, as the sun was setting most dramatically, the Captain would toss whatever orange-clad manual or textbook he'd found that day into the sea. The manuals, and the crew members that had preceded the Captain's reign, were stubbornly persistent. Every day he would be confronted by one of these latent crew members, many of them women-not-wearing-bathing-suits, and they would tell him he was doing things that were against the rules of the ship, and with them they would have a large orange binder, full of regulations and rules—much like the one his daughter had found in the early days. Every time he would have to call the Snowmen, and the Snowmen would first have to separate the crew member from the orange manual, and then separate the crew member from the ship, therefore separating that crew member's everlasting spirit from their corporeal form. Then the Captain would toss the orange binder overboard, too, wishing it would sink but watching as instead it stayed afloat, drifting out of view in the *Glory*'s white wake.

During the wee hours, the Snowmen would knock on the doors of Certain People, and the friends of Certain People, pounding furiously on their cabin doors and telling them to watch out, to beware, that they were next, and to sleep well in the meantime. Many of the Certain People did not sleep well, though, and decided to end their lives before being thrown into the sea. So they self-immolated, and self-opioded, and threw themselves overboard in the quiet hours. It was a time of terror and sadism unlike any the passengers of the *Glory* could recall, and it proved to the Captain and his coterie that they were really onto something.

And what were those opposed to the Captain doing all this time? After the Captain was first elected, they responded in sundry ways. Some simply figured that all captains had flaws—that there was a sameness to all captains, in that they stood on the bridge and steered and occasionally were subject to scandals and controversies and periodically had extramarital affairs with pornographic actresses while their wives were nursing their children, and chose not to pay taxes, and from time to time stole money from investors in failed businesses, and denigrated vast swaths of the population, and incited violence against Certain People and ended many lives in horrific ways, and threatened friendly ships and admired enemy ships, and appointed known felons and sociopaths to positions of power, and that all of it was a wash, and none of it was all that important vis-à-vis their own complicated lives that were also full of weakness and contradiction, even if not full of pornographic actresses.

Then there were others, who were so shattered by the idea that the noble ship *Glory,* with its august history and towering ideals and intellectual achievements, had chosen a base charlatan to lead it. These passengers, who might be called idealists, or at least optimists, usually saw the best in their fellow passengers, and were so shocked and disappointed in the Most Foul that even many weeks after the Captain's ascendance, they were still catatonic. For them, seeing their neighbors and friends and even relatives wearing chicken costumes and cheering the Captain's evisceration of every law and large-hearted idea ever conceived on the *Glory,* not to mention the Most Foul's cheering of the ritual drowning of other humans aboard, was so soul-rupturing that they could scarcely get out of bed.

Finally, there were the passengers who chose to fight the Captain and the Upskirt Boys, and they did so whenever they could. They called themselves the Kindly Mutineers, for they were determined not to stoop to the base level of the Captain and Snowmen and the Most Foul. Instead they rebelled politely, with properly filled-out complaint forms and sternly worded memos. When these forms and memos had no effect—the Captain had the Snowmen burn them each night, upon a pyre, around which the feathered Most Foul danced—the Kindly Mutineers then filed injunctions and passed resolutions. When these injunctions and resolutions had no effect, they looked in the few remaining ship's manuals, which contained the ship's laws and regulations, to see if the Captain had violated any of them. Very quickly they realized that the Captain had violated many hundreds of these laws and regulations—had in fact violated all but a few of them with astonishing speed and thoroughness.

Having realized this, though, the Kindly Mutineers were unsure what step to take next. It seemed very drastic to unseat the Captain, and to be sure, trying to unseat him carried with it the risk of failure, given the fact that he had many supporters dressed as birds. The passengers dressed as birds had voted him Captain, the Kindly Mutineers reasoned, and perhaps it was not right to unseat the Captain the bird-people had elected, just because he had violated the ship's every rule and had sanctioned the murder of upwards of 122 or so humans via drowning, many of them succumbing to the seas while the Most Foul chanted things like "Drown the Brown!" and "Dunk the Punk."

This had become a thing. The Most Foul had found that they very much liked to chant. They liked to chant whatever the Captain suggested they chant, and they also liked to make up their own chants, one of which was "Drown the Brown," which they created for the occasions when Certain People—whose skin color tended toward brown—were thrown overboard. When they saw the Snowmen take a Certain Person from their cabins or workplaces or the infirmary, the Most Foul would gather at the railing and watch the Snowmen swing the human to and fro, by the arms and legs, before flinging them over the ship's edge. All the while, the Most Foul would chant "Drown the Brown!" if the Certain Person was brown, and "Dunk the Punk!" if that brown person was also a child. And when the person had dropped into the ocean and sunk to the seafloor, never again to think or see or love, the Most Foul would return to their rooms and watch television.

The Kindly Mutineers could not deduce what had happened to their shipmates. Either the Most Foul, with whom they peacefully had shared the *Glory* for years—before they began calling themselves by this new name—had always been secretly bloodthirsty, waiting for the opportunity to watch others die, or something about the Captain had created a hot crimson fever, had awoken a long-dormant contagion of ugliness and casual barbarism. The Kindly Mutineers had hope, however faint, that it was indeed a fever that had possessed their fellow passengers, and, like any fever, it would eventually break.

In the meantime, though, the Kindly Mutineers thought hard about what to do to save the lives of the remaining Certain People, and perhaps save the soul of the *Glory*. They decided to send a carrier pigeon across the ocean to beckon forth the one person who knew what to do in a situation like this. They sent for the Sheriff of the Seas.

The Sheriff of the Seas was a bit of a legend and something of a myth. He was an unassailable lawman who could be called upon when justice needed rendering and when the oppressed had exhausted every other option and hope. The one catch with the Sheriff of the Seas was that he was mute, or pretended to be mute in order to increase his mystique. In any case, whenever he rendered justice, he did so in the form of many-paged summaries of wrongdoing which were researched exhaustively and worded carefully, but which required the local persons to both read these summaries and to use these summaries in their own ways in order to exact justice. It was known that all through this process of research and fact-finding, the Sheriff worked silently and provided no updates or hints, which only enhanced his aura and terrified his quarry.

A few weeks after the pigeon flew away, the Kindly Mutineers got word, via a different carrier pigeon—long story—that the Sheriff of the Seas would be coming. The Kindly Mutineers were jubilant, and they sent yet another carrier pigeon—very long story, sorry—back to the Sheriff, telling him to arrive under cover of night, for the Captain would otherwise have his Snowmen do nasty things to him, or even worse.

One night, when a gray fog had overtaken the horizon, the Kindly Mutineers found that the Sheriff was already aboard. Somehow in the fog he had managed to sail up to the *Glory,* board, and set up an office in a location he would not disclose even to the Mutineers. He was tall and gaunt and had a way of walking, angled forward and with his chin tucked into his chest, that implied he was forever confronting a strong wind. And true to legend, he was mute. He said nothing to them, only shook their hands, listened to their concerns, and disappeared again into the fog.

After many weeks of rigorous work, the Sheriff presented the Kindly Mutineers his findings via a thousand-page tome. The manuscript was scrupulous and detailed and impossible to refute, and though it was dense, on every other page the Sheriff had made clear, in plain language, in language all children and many inanimate objects could understand, the towering crimes the Captain had committed. These crimes were so numerous and so grievous that the Sheriff was quite sure that the Captain would not only be relieved of his duties, but would likely be sent to the brig for the remainder of his years. He handed this report to the representative of the Kindly Mutineers and turned to be on his way.

"Hold on a sec," this representative said. The Kindly Mutineers had elected among their members a leader, who acted as spokesperson, and even a kind of shadow captain. She was known to be a master negotiator and a brilliant tactician and thus had been nicknamed the Wily Strategist.

"Before you go," she said to the Sheriff, holding the report in her two hands, and making a frowny-face to indicate how heavy she found the book, "can you give us the gist?"

The Sheriff said nothing, for he was mute, or pretended to be mute (for it really did increase his mystique). He put his long wrinkled forefinger on the cover of the book the Strategist held, and raised his thick eyebrows in a way that strongly implied that the answers were within its pages.

"Are you saying we should read this book?" she asked the Sheriff. The Sheriff did not answer; instead he tapped the book again with his long wrinkled forefinger and again did his thing with the eyebrows.

"Are you saying the answers are inside?" she asked.

The Sheriff felt that nodding was a form of speech, and he considered himself mute, or at least mute-curious, so again he worked his eyebrows up and down, turned and left, never to be seen again.

The Kindly Mutineers gathered around the book he had left them. One of their members touched it, and then jumped back, sucking his fingers. Another member used a stick to lift its cover, but quickly grew scared and hid under a table. The Kindly Mutineers circled the intimidating text for hours, making quivery approaches and rabbity retreats. No one wanted to open it. No one did.

"I think we're doing the right thing," the Strategist said, and so they did nothing.

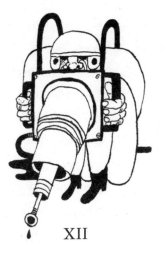

XII

FOR AVA, LIFE was perhaps more confusing than for most passengers on the *Glory*. Before the ascendance of the Captain, she had extolled the virtues of virtue, only to see her fellow passengers, the ostensible adults aboard, give all their earthly power to a man they all knew to be cretinous, erratic, nihilistic and dim. After the election, she had returned home to find a giant chicken in her family's cabin. It was her own father, dressed in the garb of the Most Foul. "Honey," he said, and held out his feathered arms. "We needed a change."

Her mother sat next to her father, rolling her eyes.

"Your father," she said, "is a moron for the time being. But we can agree to disagree, and we can love each other still."

Ava fled, disbelieving, feeling betrayed and lost. She wandered the ship in a state of catatonia that lasted weeks.

When she returned, she found her father in his usual chair, though his eyes were icy and inanimate.

"They took her," he said. "The Snowmen. She was Certain. I should have known."

Ava screamed. She circled the ship screaming. She screamed until she could no longer scream or stand or breathe, and finally she returned to the door to her family's cabin, knowing that her mother was gone and all she had left was her father, who at least she knew, now, would have regained his senses. When she opened the door, though, he was still sitting where she'd left him, and was still dressed as a chicken.

"Laws are laws," he said, his voice steady and distant. He then talked at length about what he and his motherless daughter would do with the $1.50 the Captain had promised. As he mused, his eyes regained some of their life, but a thunderous knock at the door ended his reverie.

Three Snowmen burst into the room, grabbed Ava's father roughly, and stood him atop a portable scale they had brought with them. After a few *tsks* containing both disappointment and glee, the Snowmen told Ava's father that he was overweight and disgusting, and—with help from three more Snowmen—threw him over the railing.

SORRY ABOUT ORPHANS!

. . . the Captain wrote the following morning.

GET IN "SHAPE" AND LIVE LONGER :)

*

ME? ALL MY WEIGHT IN MY P-NUS.

The Captain smiled to himself after finishing the day's messages, for he knew his wit brought much happiness to his supporters, who he considered filthy animals who were generally overweight and most of whom would have to be murdered via drowning. But until that time, he knew his irreverent humor would be pleasing to the Most Foul, and would stick it to the stuffed shirts who did not appreciate public discussion of his penis, or got weepy at the thought of orphaned children.

All in all, the Captain was having a wonderful time, even though every day brought new challenges. Though the Captain and the Snowmen had made it clear that there was no room for Certain People on the ship, new people of the Certain People type continued to approach the *Glory* via dinghy and junk and raft, and these people had to be dissuaded. The Captain thought cannon fire a practical solution, and for a time, he had the Snowmen destroy the vessels and their humans in this manner.

67

But soon the Captain was apprised of the great expense and scarcity of cannonballs, so the Snowmen suggested the ship's many water cannons as an alternative. These water cannons used ocean water and then directed it, at a hundred miles an hour, at anyone below. The Captain was delighted by this device, and asked the Snowmen to demonstrate it on what seemed to be a family of five, desperate and emaciated, arriving in a tiny tin fishing boat. The Snowmen directed a plume of water, thousands of gallons of it, at the tiny tin boat, and instantly the family was drenched, made invisible by the force and volume of water. The figure that seemed to be the father—hard to see from so high up—soon fell into the ocean and then the mother, holding a baby, followed him into the sea. The two remaining figures, who appeared to be elderly and frail, held on for a few more seconds, but then their tin boat capsized—it almost spun, which the Captain thought beautiful, in a way, the way the silver took the light—flinging the humans left and right, and the boat sank, and the family sank shortly thereafter. The Captain was impressed. This water-cannon method was efficient, cost-effective, and, to those who enjoyed witnessing suffering from a safe distance, entertaining, too. So much so that he began charging people to watch it.

Indeed, when the Captain was elevated to the *Glory*'s highest office, the Upskirt Boys had seen this as not only very funny and actually hilarious and maybe surreal—certainly the craziest thing that had happened in their lifetimes or perhaps in the history of ships or democracy—they also saw it as a great opportunity to make a buck.

Using the public bathrooms on the ship had always been free, but Ed the Unwashed set up turnstiles in front of every toilet and urinal and charged the passengers on a sliding scale depending on the density, volume and mass of their discharge. Fingers took over the ship's schools and daycare, both of which had previously been free, and charged for both, according to the children's density, volume, mass, and the attractiveness of their mothers. Sweetie sold the children's candy—which Fingers continued to steal—back to them at a reasonable rate, prime plus three. Patsy the Murderer and Paul the Manafort charged passengers to walk on the promenades and swim in the pool and walk through doorways and use silverware and look at the sunsets and breathe air.

The Most Foul were happy to pay all these fees, knowing that the Captain had put an extra $1.50 in their pockets. They had not seen this extra $1.50 yet, because the Captain had not given it to them and in fact had forgotten he'd promised to, but the Most Foul continued to throw him rallies at least once a week, during which they would dress in their feathers and beaks and cheer whatever he said. They would cheer the people thrown overboard, and cheer the marvel of the new water cannon that killed people, and they would cheer the fact that the Captain was their Captain, and had not changed at all since becoming captain.

They loved that he said things like "Liquidate the poor," which they wanted to say, too, even though many of them were poor, and they loved that he said things like "Let's put away and polish off Certain People who come from tiny pathetic boats," which they wanted to say, too, even though the ancestors, or even parents, of every last one of them had come from tiny pathetic boats, too. Most of all they loved that he did not change, and continued to say anything that popped into his head. Just that morning, on the wipe-away board, he had threatened to start a war with a country that had always been very friendly with the *Glory* and had then reversed himself in the afternoon. No doubt about it—that was shaking things up! The Most Foul had feared, in their most secret hearts, that the man with the yellow feather, once captain, would become dignified and dull, but he had been captain for months now, and was just as unvarnished, unrehearsed, and unhinged as ever, and this made them very happy and very proud. They had not foreseen the towering cruelty and daily drownings of innocents, the putting-away and polishing-off, but this additional part of life on the *Glory,* though horrifying and against every belief system and moral code ever devised by humans, was new, and anything new was something different, and different was inherently good.

XIII

AND YET, EVEN after these rallies, the Captain lived with a certain emptiness. His daughter was spending more and more time playing with her vacant-eyed doll, and because she was now styling herself as a feminist icon, she had designed a new line of push-up bras and high-heeled shoes. Thus the Captain often found himself alone on the bridge, and though he could, if so inspired, add new defacements to the portraits of past captains, there was a missing piece in his life, a hole in the shape of a man.

Then, on the horizon, he saw the happiest of sights: the crimson sails of the Pale One, one of the sea's most notorious and feared pirates, a man who had been the stated enemy of the *Glory* for as long as anyone could remember, in part because he had tried to end the *Glory*—with cannons, with

71

guns, with undersea saboteurs and a new kind of sonic weapon that made people's eardrums bleed—more times than anyone could remember.

There was no way to quantify the admiration the Captain had for the Pale One. He liked the way the Pale One was built, and how he carried himself, and how impressive he looked while riding a horse, and how masculine he looked without a shirt, and he liked especially how phenomenally masculine and impressive the Pale One looked without a shirt while riding a horse. He liked how the Pale One did business, liked particularly the way he murdered his enemies, or ordered the murder of his enemies—in the light of day, and in the most innovative ways. The Pale One used pestiferous gas on his critics and had exposed other adversaries to slow-acting toxins that caused the victims to age decades in months before finally expiring. And sometimes he simply sent his armies into foreign lands to subjugate their people and loot everything of value. The Pale One was undeniably a go-getter with a knack for making things happen.

"Captain," said a voice. The Captain looked around him to find a woman wearing a white uniform decorated with medals and epaulets. Though the Captain had been dismissing people every day since he took command of the ship, every day another crew member came out of the woodwork, each of them carrying a clipboard and offering unsolicited advice.

It was maddening. And this inversion of the natural order—uniforms were for men, bathing suits for women—gave him a kind of vertigo. He closed his eyes, hoping this would cause her to disappear, but her voice announced her persistence.

"Surely you don't plan to invite the Pale One aboard the ship?" the woman said. "He's known as one of the great villains of the world, a treacherous fiend who gasses his own people and is the ally of other fiends and blackguards—"

The Captain called the Snowmen, who burst in and took this woman-not-wearing-a-bathing-suit away. While they were throwing her over the railing, the Captain rushed to the bathroom to freshen up, because in the looks department, the Pale One was no slouch, and legend had it he always smelled musky and clean.

While the Captain was in the bathroom, the Snowmen, after being sure that the woman had drowned thoroughly in the *Glory*'s frothy wake, saw the red sails of the Pale One's ship approaching and sounded the ship's alarms. Cannons were loaded, guns were aimed, and the ship's passengers all observed emergency procedures, given the Pale One and his murderous band had been the stated enemies of the ship for as long as anyone could remember.

When the Captain emerged from the bathroom, having tried a new aftershave he thought very manly but with a hint of jasmine, he saw the ship in an uproar. He panicked for a second, hoping that all the hullabaloo wouldn't be seen by the Pale One, who was now within striking distance and who he did not want to offend.

"Stand down!" the Captain said into the intercom, and then explained that the Pale One, whose crimes against the *Glory* were too many to name or number, was actually his personal friend and should be treated as such.

For many of the passengers on the ship, this was very confusing information. It was known that the Pale One had waged war on the *Glory* and, during that war, had captured and tortured the Admiral. It was known that the Pale One regularly murdered women who loved women and men who loved men. It was known that the Pale One spent much of his time lending a hand to the worst despots on sea and land, arriving just in time to help them overthrow duly elected leaders and murder innocent civilians and occasionally eat them, too, adding a special sauce, spicy but not too spicy, that he'd created himself.

As the Pale One's ship got closer, the passengers of the *Glory* could see that its sails were a faded red; legend had it that they had been dyed that way with the blood of orphans. They could see that dozens of oars extended from the hull; it was assumed that these rowers were slaves. Trailing from the Pale One's ship were seven long frayed ropes, each attached to a small wooden boat, big enough for one human, and in each of these boats was indeed one human, each human handcuffed and hog-tied, and most of these humans now dead and decomposing.

As the Pale One's ship pulled up alongside the *Glory,* the Captain stood on the bow, waving wildly, bouncing on his tiptoes, his face overcome by a toothy grin of boundless joy. "Welcome!" he yelled as the Pale One's blood-soaked sails were lowered and the ship turned slowly to tie up.

"Welcome!" echoed the Most Foul, who had gathered on the railings in full-feathered regalia.

The Pale One's crew threw a rope over the rail, and a gangway was lowered. The first of the Pale One's minions strode onto the *Glory,* carrying muskets and machetes and also hundreds of empty sacks, the kind commonly used for looting and pillaging. Without a word, they immediately fanned out, disappearing into every corner of the vessel.

And finally the Pale One himself appeared. The Captain almost fainted, for, as he hoped, the Pale One was shirtless, and was sitting astride a horse, and the horse, carrying the Pale One, walked majestically aboard the *Glory,* and then, once on deck, dropped a monumental mound of feces onto the head of a small child dressed by his parents in Most Foul feathers.

"Welcome!" the Captain said and they shook hands, and the Captain's knees went weak. The Pale One's hand was just as smooth as he had hoped, and just as strong—like steel wrapped in chamois. The Pale One dismounted with an ironic smile, his tiny ice-blue eyes never looking directly at the Captain, or indeed at anyone or anything. His mouth was locked into a perpetual smirk, and whatever was in front of him, his eyes were elsewhere.

The Captain was so nervous! The Pale One was so much more impressive in person, and indeed he smelled fantastic—far muskier than the Captain had the temerity to hope.

"Won't you join me in the stateroom for a cheeseburger?" he asked the Pale One, and when the Pale One agreed, and when the Pale One was actually following him through the *Glory,* just the two of them on their way to the Captain's chambers, the Captain thought he might swoon. He'd wanted everything to be perfect, so he had ordered his favorite food in great quantities. When he opened the stateroom door, he swelled with pride, taking in the table stacked high not only with cheeseburgers prepared by teenagers and wrapped in thin paper, but also hamburgers prepared by teenagers and wrapped in thin paper of a different color.

Upon seeing the table stacked high with cheeseburgers prepared by teenagers and wrapped in thin paper, the Pale One smirked and looked elsewhere. The Captain quickly became flustered. He thought of topics they could discuss.

His daughter? He tried to think of where he might have a nice picture of his daughter. He considered calling his daughter in. She always knew what to say, or at least knew how to wear a sexy number that did all the talking.

The Captain decided he should just speak his heart, so he confessed his admiration for the Pale One, at how the Pale One steered his ship, how he commanded his people, and how he occasionally murdered his enemies in creative ways involving rare toxins.

"You are making me blush," the Pale One said, though he did not blush, and had never blushed.

"Speaking of enemies. . . ," the Captain said, and then paused. He did not want to seem like a novice at the disposing of adversaries, but he did want advice for the disposal of people like the woman-not-wearing-a-bathing-suit who had advised against welcoming the Pale One. Throwing her overboard was effective as a way to be rid of her, but it did not necessarily send a lasting message to other crew members who might get mouthy in the future.

"There *is* a better way," the Pale One said, and his mouth bent into something like a smile. He then pointed to the rear of his ship, to which the seven long frayed ropes had been tied, each of them leading to a small wooden boat containing a dying or dead human.

"All of these people disappointed me and proved useless, but now," the Pale One said with a coquettish smile, "they are quite useful."

The Captain whistled aloud. He slapped the table with both palms. He considered reaching over and touching the Pale One's hand in a gesture of admiration and friendship, but decided against it. Instead he simply said, "That's why you're the Pale One."

"Again you make me blush," the Pale One said, though he did not blush, and never had blushed.

XIV

THE PALE ONE and his men settled in. They were given their own rooms and all the food they wanted. They roamed the ship, taking pictures of the bridge and of the engine room, and occasionally they robbed the ship's passengers, killed men over minor disagreements, and kidnapped and raped women and children. The Captain couldn't recall a better time of his life. He and the Pale One had wonderful evenings during which the Captain ate cheeseburgers and sodas and the Pale One ate nothing, instead telling the Captain remarkable stories of times he had imposed his will on subjects both unwilling and worshipful.

At the encouragement of the Pale One, every day the Captain would think of new people who he could handcuff, put on leaky boats and drag behind the *Glory*. The Captain put the former chief engineer in such a boat, and the former navigator, and the former cruise director. All three were in small boats bouncing around amid the frothing wake of the powerful ship, handcuffed and helpless and waiting to die.

"It's more satisfying than simple drowning, no?" the Pale One said. The Captain and the Pale One were standing on the bridge, and it was sunset, and the Captain felt, for only the second time in his life, that he really had a friend. He'd do anything for the Pale One, and in a burst of gratitude and affection, he told him so.

"Yes, I know," the Pale One said, while his eyes were looking elsewhere. "But you have already done too much for me. Now I want to do something for you."

"What is it?" the Captain asked, his heart fluttering like a sparrow's.

"It will be a surprise," the Pale One said. "You will find out in the morning."

And indeed it was a surprise! The Captain awoke to yet another crew member, yet another woman-not-wearing-a-bathing-suit, informing him that the Pale One's men had put every member of the Upskirt Boys in small leaky boats trailing the *Glory,* and that some of them were already dead. Fingers was dead, for he had had a stroke from the shock of being put in such a boat; his corpse was being pecked at by the seabirds, now carnivorous, who had developed a taste for human flesh while following the ship and its many decomposing bodies. Freddie the Whack and Ed the Unwashed and Pasty the Murderer and of course Paul the Manafort were all trailing the *Glory,* bouncing helplessly in the wake, handcuffed and waiting to die. Sweetie and Pete the Pipe, who the Captain understood to be close friends of the Pale One, were now dead and dismembered and their many parts were arranged in a small pyramidal pile on a small raft, their heads on top like sundae cherries.

"Surprise!" the Pale One said as he entered the bridge.

When the Captain asked the Pale One why he had sent all of his friends to such a fate, the Pale One's answer was very sound: "You had too much middle management," he said, and the Captain knew he was right.

"Also, we killed all the crew in the engine room," the Pale One said. As if to answer the Captain's next question, he said, "But do not worry. My men have it under control."

Thinking about his many feelings—concern for all his friends, who were now dead or dying, and happiness that the engine-room crew was no longer—the Captain decided that, on balance, all of this was wonderful news.

"You are phenomenal," the Captain said.

"You make me blush," the Pale One said, while not blushing. "But there is more. Close your eyes."

The Captain closed his eyes and heard the distinctive sound of a ship approaching. His mind raced, thinking who this visitor could be.

"Can we go see?" he asked the Pale One, and the Pale One smiled slyly while looking elsewhere. The Captain, feeling very much like a child on Christmas morning, ran to the rail to see who was arriving. When he saw the symbol on the topsail—two swords intersecting below a severed head—he knew it was Bloodbeard, one of the ocean's most loathed and feared pirates, a known proponent of hangings and stonings and especially beheadings. It was his penchant for the latter that had given him his nickname, for after each beheading, which he performed himself, Bloodbeard used his beard to wipe the blood off his sword. It was quite an effect.

"Surprise again," the Pale One said. The two of them stood on the deck, ready to welcome Bloodbeard, whose crew was, at the moment, tying their ship to the *Glory*. Bloodbeard's crew, all of whom wore purple clothing and stylish black masks, lowered the gangway, and strode across onto the *Glory* fully armed with swords and daggers, and quickly disappeared into the ship, carrying empty sacks, the kind commonly used for looting and also pillaging.

They were followed by eight men, all wearing gold-trimmed tunics and carrying Bloodbeard himself on a golden litter. The Captain gasped. Bloodbeard wore a gold-trimmed robe, and some kind of golden helmet, and even golden gloves. Immediately the Captain was ashamed he had not thought of a gold-trimmed robe and golden helmet and golden gloves for himself, and made a mental note to put someone on a wooden boat as punishment for this oversight. Once Bloodbeard had been carried onto the *Glory,* he was lowered to the deck. He stood up, at which point the Captain gasped again and made another wooden-boat note. Bloodbeard was wearing golden socks! And golden shoes! Each with a golden tassel!

Now the Captain saw that Bloodbeard was holding, in one of his golden-gloved hands, what appeared to be a wire birdcage covered in golden cloth. Bloodbeard put the birdcage down and turned to the Pale One, whereupon the two of them exchanged a hearty handshake that was much like a high five, in that it was high, but it was also a handshake, and it was very forceful and hard, such that when their hands came together, they made a very loud and satisfying clapping sound that filled the Captain with both awe and envy. The Captain wondered how he might ask about the handshake, how he might learn it, and thought he could do this once the three of them were alone in his stateroom. He was about to suggest they retire there when the Pale One preempted him.

"Let's go to the Captain's stateroom," he said, with a funny, perhaps even ironic, emphasis on the word *Captain,* while smiling and looking at Bloodbeard, who smiled a toothy and knowing smile. They all walked toward the stateroom, the Captain finding himself trailing behind the two of them, Bloodbeard and the Pale One engaged in a very intimate and loving and laugh-filled discussion as they walked down the *Glory*'s hallways. Periodically one or the other of them would point a thumb back in the direction of the Captain, and if the Captain were not so self-assured and strong, he would have thought the two of them enjoying many jokes at his expense, but this could not be, he assured himself, because he was self-assured, and also he was the Captain, and he had a legion of people backing him every step of the way while dressed as chickens.

When they entered the stateroom, the Pale One and Bloodbeard found a spectacular spread of cheeseburgers wrapped in thin paper, all of them prepared by teenagers. Upon seeing this, the Pale One turned to Bloodbeard and said, "I told you! I told you!" To which Bloodbeard turned to the Pale One and said, "You told me! You told me!" And then the two of them clapped their hands again in that wonderful hard and high clapping handshake they had done before, and then they laughed for what seemed to the Captain like ten minutes, but was actually far longer.

XV

THAT NIGHT, THE CAPTAIN lay under his bed and had a fitful sleep. At one point he had the strange feeling that the ship was turning almost completely around.

Then he had a terrible dream. He was still the captain, and still on the bridge, but the *Glory* was sailing through the thickest of fogs. He tried to turn the wheel, but it would not turn. Nothing he did had any effect whatsoever on the steering. It was as if the ship was being pulled inexorably toward some object by some unseen force. And indeed it was, for out of the fog came the silver sails for which the Admiral was known. The sails seemed to reach for the Captain, pulling him toward them with irresistible force.

In the dream, the Admiral's distinctive silver sails were coming through the white mist with horrible and deliberate

85

speed. The Captain tried to turn but nothing worked. He put all his considerable weight on the wheel but it had no effect. The silver sails came toward him until he was surrounded by them, by their blinding light. The Admiral's small dark eyes stared into him with unnerving resolve, imploring him, without a word, to be better.

The Captain felt his teeth loosen and crumble; they fell from his gums and were like pebbles in his mouth. He spit them out but his tongue came with them. When he tried to scream, he made no sound. He reached for his throat but when he lifted his hands, his fingers broke, one by one, like dried clay, leaving stubs that dissolved, disappearing like ash in a gale. He looked in horror at his handless arms, and, thinking he could outrun the disassembly of his body, he put one foot forward, then the other, but both buckled, bent, and snapped off like cheap plastic.

Without feet, his ankles could not support him and he dropped to his knees, which turned to wet putty, sending his torso soaring forward and his face plunging toward the ground. And here time slowed. This part of the dream, when his head was speeding to the earth, and all the while he knew that when it struck the hard ground it would shatter, seemed to last for hours. And while his head was flying downward, all the while he sensed the Admiral watching him, without malice and yet without compassion.

The Captain woke with a start. He was soaked through and drooling, his hands were trembling, his nose was running. He'd been crying, too.

"Hello?" he said into the vent. "You there?"

After a pause the voice answered, "Of course I am."

"Do you think I'm brave?" the Captain asked.

From the vent there was a brief fit of coughs and throat clearings. Finally the voice said, "The bravest!"

This buoyed the Captain somewhat, but he pressed on. "The Admiral fought in the war and everyone says he was courageous. Do you think people think I'm a coward just because I hid in the bowels of the ship, looking at pornographic magazines?"

"Listen," the voice in the vent said. "No one really cares about who fought in that war. And just about everyone likes pornography."

The Captain laughed through his tears, knowing that again the voice in the vent had spoken an undeniable truth that assuaged his most private doubts.

"And I know this sounds silly," the Captain went on, "but sometimes I think I'm not doing enough."

The voice in the vent gasped. "No! Don't say that!"

The Captain continued, "I promised the passengers that everything would get better, but so far all I've done is write on the wipe-away board, throw a hundred and eighty-seven

87

people overboard, and promise to give the rest of the people a dollar and fify cents, which I don't think I ever did."

"Which makes you by far the greatest captain who has ever captained," the voice said. "No captain has ever done more for the ship than you."

The Captain sniffled, smiling to himself and feeling very grateful for the voice in the vent, and very proud of himself for all he had done.

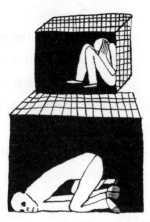

XVI

IN THE MORNING, the Captain showered and dressed and went to the bridge, only to find the door locked. He looked through the portal, and saw the Pale One standing at the steering wheel, surrounded by the Pale One's own crew, who appeared to have taken over the navigation of the ship.

"Captain!"

He turned to find Bloodbeard standing behind him, wearing an even more impressive outfit than he had the day before. While yesterday's clothes were embroidered in gold, this outfit appeared to be actually made of gold. His robe seemed very heavy, perhaps a hundred pounds or more, but Bloodbeard seemed to be wearing it lightly. He was quite a man.

"Let's go for a walk," he said to the Captain, and, putting

his arm around the Captain's rounded, fleshy shoulder, turned him from the bridge door and down the steps to the lower deck. As they descended, the Captain sensed that the ship was indeed going in the opposite direction than it had been going before he went to bed. It was as if the Pale One had taken control of the ship and turned it around completely—which seemed like just the kind of naughty surprise the Pale One would devise.

"That's a shame," Bloodbeard said. He was pointing to a small group of dinghies and junks approaching the *Glory*.

The Captain's face went hot with embarrassment. He'd been throwing people off the ship, in part to thwart the arrival of any newcomers to the *Glory*. And yet, from time to time, new boats and rafts still approached, full of desperate women and men and children. It was a disgrace.

"The problem is you're wasting a precious resource," Bloodbeard said. "You throw these people into the ocean and this sends a message to your passengers, yes, but it says nothing to those from far away who cannot see these people drown. They sink too quickly."

What was needed, Bloodbeard explained, was a constant and horrifying signal to those who might arrive by boat looking for safe haven. It was essential, he said, that those approaching would be confronted by a clear visual deterrent.

"Why do you think I carry this around?" Bloodbeard

said, indicating the covered birdcage he'd been holding since he came aboard.

The Captain did not see the connection between a pet bird and a deterrent to boat people, but he didn't know how to say this without risking looking uninformed. He positioned his lips in a serious pose meant to imply contemplation.

"Did I not show you this?" Bloodbeard said, and with a flourish removed the cloth from the birdcage. Inside was not a bird but a head. It was a man's head, severed at the neck, and appeared to have been decomposing for weeks. Seeing it, the Captain had a flicker of recognition. He'd heard something about a man who had been asking annoying questions of Bloodbeard, and then this man had disappeared. Now the Captain made the connection between the missing man and the severed head, and also made the connection between the birdcage and the visual deterrent Bloodbeard had described.

"Speaking of which," Bloodbeard said, "I noticed that you have hundreds of cages for lobsters and crabs and such."

The Captain had never seen any cages for lobsters or crabs, but then again, he'd never seen much of the ship, and did not know where its food came from. So he took Bloodbeard's word for it, and listened intently as Bloodbeard laid out a plan.

*

That afternoon, the ship's passengers, who had grown accustomed to hearing the thumping resistance of whomever the Snowmen had found and decided to throw overboard, and had become inured to the otherworldly screaming of the victims' spouses and children, were surprised to hear nothing of the kind this day. They were so curious about the lack of thumping and wailing that they peeked out of their rooms and took furtive steps toward the promenade and railings to see what was not happening.

What they found were Certain People being kept in cages meant for lobsters and crabs. These cages were placed every thirty feet or so on the outer decks, so that no passengers had to walk far from their rooms to encounter a human in a cage meant for mollusks and crustaceans. There were enough of the cages—easily ninety, on multiple decks—that any desperate vessel approaching the ship would notice the cages, would see the humans within, and would get the clear message that the ship was an unfriendly place where compassion had died and wherein reigned a towering disregard for the vulnerable and dispossessed.

"Love it," said the voice in the vent that night.

"It was Bloodbeard's idea," said the Captain.

"We're lucky to have friends like this," said the voice in the vent. "They give and they give, and they ask for nothing in return."

*

The passengers went about their lives with minor adjustments. Because the marauding crews of Bloodbeard and the Pale One regularly robbed the passengers and plundered their rooms, most passengers preferred to stay inside with their doors locked. When the brave few did venture outside, they tried to avoid the decks where the humans-in-cages were located, because even on windy days the smell of decaying flesh was very strong, and the sight and sound of the humans-in-cages—even though evidence of the Captain's decisiveness—was nevertheless hard to bear, especially when the humans-in-cages were children, with their dying wails high-pitched and feral.

Even the passengers' long-standing tradition of watching the sea, or the sunsets, or being outside for any period of time, was not the same sort of beautiful as it had been, given the three dozen or so former crew members and various enemies of the Captain trailing behind in leaky rowboats, some of them already dead and being picked apart by carrion birds and the occasional shark.

Because most of the sanitation and custodial workers had been thrown overboard or were now in traps meant for crustaceans, the boat had taken on a ragged appearance and a fetid odor. The Captain's daughter one day opened her own cabin door and noticed this smell, which seemed a hybrid of rotting flesh, despair, and stale urine, and saw an opportunity. Her forward-thinking line of push-up bras, nose-narrowers and thigh-minimizers had been a hit among the Most Foul, but—an oversight veritably insane, she realized—she had no fragrance to her name. Now the ship needed one, and she rose to the challenge, calling it Eau de Oubli and making sure, through thorough testing on Certain Children and the elderly, that it was safe for humans, and effectively masked the ship's overwhelming stench of strife and decay. Almost immediately, the scent was very popular among the dozens who could afford it. These passengers soaked their scarves in it, covering their mouths in order to walk outside, and breathed comfortably for minutes at a time.

Otherwise leaving one's cabin was unpleasant and was not often done. Which was just as well, given that most of the restaurants on board had been shuttered long ago, because the makers of these foods were Certain People and thus had been thrown overboard. The Thai place was closed. The Chinese places were closed. The Ecuadorian place was long shuttered, as were the Nepalese, Ethiopian, and Peruvian eateries. The Mexican restaurants had been closed so long they were now being used to assemble and store more cages. The one remaining food option was the cheeseburger outlet favored by the Captain. That establishment was run partially by machines and partially by teenagers, who thus were not in immediate danger of being thrown into the sea.

During the day, the passengers watched television news, the hosts of which enumerated the many dangers outside the passengers' cabins, which made the passengers' habit of staying indoors even more prudent. Because the passengers got no exercise and rarely saw the sun, they had trouble sleeping, and between their restlessness and the many fears they had of rectal-bleeding spiders and various other threats—including the remaining Certain People and of course the marauding crews of the Pale One and Bloodbeard—they, like their Captain, took to hiding under their beds, and when they did, one by one, they too discovered the voice in the vent. And like the Captain, the Most Foul found that the voice in the vent really understood them and voiced their innermost fears with great candor and insight. Between the voice in the vent, and the cheeseburgers, and staying inside paralyzed with fear, and having the *Glory* commandeered by its historic enemies and ransacked daily, and surrounded by the dead and decaying bodies of Certain People, and with no one talking to anyone else, and the only joy in anyone's life being the occasional hour when the Most Foul dressed as chickens and chanted for the deaths or jailings of their enemies, there had never been a better time.

XVII

THE CAPTAIN WOKE to the unsettling sound of the ship making a shuddering stop. He scooted out from under his bed, looked out the window and saw a thousand enormous images of the same round face. He dressed and walked to the rail and found that the *Glory* had docked at a port he'd never seen, and all around the ship, covering the docks and the surrounding town and the hillside beyond, were gigantic banners bearing the visage of a fleshy-faced man whose name the Captain could not place. He looked down and saw that a gangplank had already been extended from the *Glory,* and that a welcoming ceremony was occurring, with great pomp and circumstance, on the docks below.

The Captain changed into his most impressive military-seeming uniform, reapplied his muskiest cologne, and rushed down to the lower decks, scampering down the innumerable stairs and getting lost four or five times—for besides the bridge, he had never been anywhere on the ship but the pool, the putt-putt course, and the stairs near the women's locker room—before finally finding his way to the gangplank.

There he saw the Pale One and Bloodbeard clapping hands in their phenomenal high-five way with a man who looked very much like the man depicted in the innumerable banners all over the port and the surrounding area. These banners hung from what appeared to be human bones and, when he looked closer, the Captain was sure that the hillside was decorated with many severed heads resting on pikes. They had gone to considerable trouble to greet the *Glory,* that much was clear. So as not to insult his hosts, the Captain rushed toward the podium where the Pale One and Bloodbeard were handclapping and backslapping with the man who seemed to be the leader of this land. Just before he reached his friends, a platoon of men and women from this foreign land, dressed in drab uniforms, rushed past him and onto the *Glory,* carrying the sorts of bags commonly used for looting and pillaging. When they were gone, the Captain straightened the medals on his jacket and strode toward the gathering.

Seeing him approach, wearing his faux-military uniform, the three men—the Pale One, Bloodbeard, and the Man

So Soft, for that was the name of the one who ruled this land—looked at the Captain and all burst into uproarious laughter that seemed to the Captain to last ten minutes, but in fact lasted far longer.

They said nothing to him. When a fleet of luxurious black cars arrived, the three men got into them and drove off, none of them inviting the Captain along. For a moment or two, the Captain looked around him, catching eyes with a few of the hundred or so beheaded men and women that surrounded him, staring from their pikes. There was a certain panache to the way the Man So Soft decorated his port with the heads of his enemies, the Captain thought, but there was a certain smell, too. He wondered if his daughter's ingenious perfume would effectively disguise the odor, and wondered what kind of market there would be on this island for Eau de Oubli. He wondered, then, just where his daughter was, and thought he might go back to the *Glory* to find her and talk about this new market for her scent and really her whole brand, given all the proles he'd seen so far were short and ugly and surely would admire a sun-haired Valkyrie like her—when a rickshaw driver huffed toward him and offered him a ride.

"Follow the Man So Soft?" he asked the Captain.

The Captain worried that his friends had abandoned him, had in fact *meant* to leave him by the docks, but this seemed implausible. Still, he had to muster all of his courage, as much courage as he had mustered when he had hidden for years in the bowels of the ship looking at pornography, before finally agreeing. He stepped into the rickshaw, and the driver, trying to move the vehicle now that it bore the Captain's considerable weight, let out a high helpless squeak. Soon, though, the driver found his pace, which was far slower than the Captain or any biped could have walked himself, and it took all day for them to make their way up the many switchbacks on the densely populated hillside. Along the way they got a comprehensive cultural immersion into the nation, seeing first a thousand or so peasants plowing a landfill with their fingers, looking for food remnants or tinfoil, then a prison for children, then a very intriguing operation where the bodies of journalists were ground into a kind of paste fed to cattle. Finally, just before they reached the Man So Soft's impressive estate, there was a delightful petting zoo full of adorable goats and llamas being fed, the rickshaw driver explained, the entrails of the Man So Soft's ex-wife and former treasury secretary.

When they arrived at the Palace of the Man So Soft, which bore those words in neon above its brutalist facade, the Captain argued with the rickshaw driver over the fare, and finally paid the driver half of what the man asked for.

He rang the bell and a servant welcomed him inside and promptly brought him to a grand dining hall, bright with chandelier light and smelling of wine and meat and the sweat of perhaps forty revelers dining. Among them were his friends Bloodbeard and the Pale One, both of whom were seated near the Man So Soft. Next to the Man So Soft was a gorgeous woman, blond and curvy, drinking champagne out of an extraordinarily tall glass and looking very intrigued by her host, laughing and touching his forearm most flirtatiously, and once or twice feeding him from a long and dainty fork. The Captain thought this woman captivating and alluring, and he, too, wanted to be fed by her from a long and dainty fork, and only wanted these things more when he realized that this was his daughter.

"Hello!" he said and waved to her, but she did not see him. The Captain wanted to notify her, and the Man So Soft, and his friends the Pale One and Bloodbeard, that he had arrived, but he was quickly ushered to a very small table, in the corner of the room, where a number of children, or very diminutive and youthful-looking adults, sat eating pizza and chicken nuggets and drinking Sprite.

The Captain was hungry, and all these things looked delicious, so he ate his pizza and chicken nuggets while puzzling over exactly where he was, and who the many dozens of men and women were who surrounded the Man So Soft at the larger table. They were a formidable bunch. There were more than a few eye patches, many visible facial scars, one man who seemed to be eating the brains of a monkey with a tiny spoon, and a pair of fearsome men sharing a plate of human fingers. There were brigands and buccaneers, baby-slayers, thieves and malefactors—in short, a feast of go-getters who the Captain instinctively feared and admired. Periodically, the Captain thought he saw some of these impressive people at this larger, longer table look his way and laugh uproariously, but he could not be sure.

He tried again to get his daughter's attention, but either she did not see him or she was too enamored with the Man So Soft, who was touching her hair a great deal, much in the way an infant would touch a bearskin rug. Sometime in the middle of the meal, a show began, starting with terrified-looking acrobats, followed by a hundred or so terrified-looking singers in bright-colored traditional dresses, and ending with a small puppet or doll-man, more terrified-looking than all the others, who was made to dance atop the table while the guests threw fruit, animal bones, forks and knives at him. Given the timeless appeal of audience participation, this part of the show was far and away the most popular and many encores were demanded and performed. The Captain had a sense that this doll was his daughter's doll, but he could not be sure, for he had never paid close attention to her hobbies and companions, unless those companions were young women with luxurious hair who would let him watch them eat salad.

Speaking of salad, the Captain was gratified that the Man So Soft did not try to offer him, or any of the small children at his small table, salad. Instead, after the Captain finished his chicken nuggets and pizza and Sprite, he was given a wonderful dessert of cake pops and whipped cream, which kept him intensely occupied for a long while—so long, in fact, that when he looked up, he saw that the longer, larger table was empty and he was alone. All that was left of the great table's great feast was a human corpse, which had been hollowed out and which had been used to hold a vast sea of guacamole. Fragments of tortilla chips, a favorite of the Man So Soft, emerged from it like sails in a viscous green sea. This was like so many things the Captain had seen that day, and so many things he'd learned from the Pale One and Bloodbeard—brilliant ways of punishing, disposing of and reusing lesser humans that, while admirable and innovative, left the Captain feeling, in his most private of hearts, a bit outclassed by the Man So Soft and by his ribald dinner guests, even by the Pale One and Bloodbeard. The Captain could passively bear the suffering of anyone, could watch numbly the deaths of dozens or hundreds, but actively conjuring such creative human destruction? He was out of his league. The human-as-hollow-chip-dip-vessel? It was on another plane entirely.

Dispirited and soul-shaken, and feeling a bit bloaty from the cake pops, the Captain wandered the great halls of the Man So Soft's palace, sometimes hearing what he thought was the echoing laughter of Bloodbeard or the Pale One, once even hearing what he was sure was his daughter's distinct guffaw, but the more he walked, the more alone and less oriented he became, until he found himself in a basement storage room of some kind. He stood high on the steps, and watched what seemed to be many dozens of men and women in uniform arriving in the storage room with various things that looked quite a lot like the things he'd seen on the *Glory*. The silverware looked familiar, as did the crystal decanters and ovens and pots and pans and tables and televisions and barrels of rum and wine and whiskey. Soon these workers were carrying in what seemed to be complex machinery, and gauges, and piping, and parts of engines, and then whole engines, and finally lifeboats, all of which bore the distinctive logo of the *Glory*.

One of the workers saw the Captain standing there, mouth agape, watching their work, and this worker shooed him away, and the Captain apologized and quickly departed. He continued to wander the mansion, seeing no one he knew and feeling increasingly forsaken and longing for the comfort of the voice in the vent or the people cheering him while wearing chicken costumes. He was about to leave the mansion and find his way back to the *Glory* when three men in uniform knocked him unconscious with a series of blows to the head and neck, dragged him back to the ship and up the gangplank, threw him hastily inside, closed the hatch, and cut the *Glory* loose.

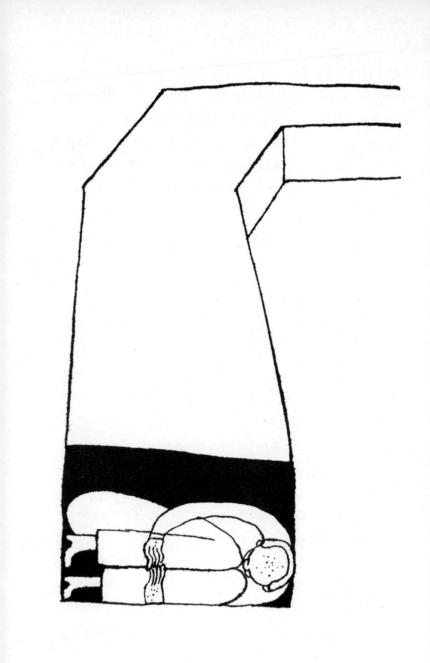

XVIII

THE PASSENGERS OF the *Glory* awoke to the unmistakable feeling of drift. They looked out their cabin windows and saw that there was no land in sight, nothing in any direction. The familiar vibration of the ship's engines had ceased, too, leaving the ship eerily silent.

Though all of the *Glory*'s passengers feared the smell of Certain People decaying in cages, and the Most Foul feared Certain People who might still be at large, all of the passengers of the *Glory,* one by one, left their cabins to find out what was happening and where they'd gone.

The ship had been stripped bare of anything of value. Everything that was not nailed down had been taken, and everything that had been nailed down had been freed of those nails and taken, too. The furniture was gone, the electronics were gone, the food and drink were gone, the putt-putt golf course was gone, and somehow the thieves had managed to steal the swimming pool and the waterslide, too. The ship was as bare as a cupboard.

"Anchor's gone," a passenger said.

"Everything on the bridge is gone, too," said another passenger, this one still dressed as a chicken.

The passengers fanned out and found that all the ship's navigation equipment, that which the Captain hadn't removed himself, had been stolen. There was no radar, no computers, no charts, no maps. A woman in scuba gear and flippers appeared on the deck.

"They swiped the rudder, too," she said.

The passengers looked everywhere, but they could not find the Captain. All the electrical fixtures and wires had been removed by the minions of the Man So Soft, so the lower levels and inner portions of the ship were utterly without light. The passengers fashioned torches from broomsticks and towels and they went deep into the *Glory,* looking for the Captain. Their crackling amber flames illuminated every darkened hallway, and everywhere they found the ship gutted, stripped, cleaned out.

"I bet the engines are gone," one passenger said.

The engines had indeed been removed, piece by piece, leaving, in the engine room, only the skeletal remains of the crew murdered, weeks ago—it seemed like years—by the Pale One's men. Then a whimpering was heard. It was coming from somewhere in the bowels of the ship, and the sound carried through the empty iron passageways and air ducts. The searchers meandered through these darkest and dankest parts of the *Glory,* following this most frightened and frail whining, until they came upon its source.

There was a man hiding in a vent. He was crouched down, clutching his knees, wearing a blue suit and red tie and brown loafers. He had a vast plain of sickly forehead and his black turf of hair was rapidly retreating. He looked like the kind of man who might have gone to Santa Monica High School, who might have been excluded once or twice in that large and diverse school, and who, trying one last time to win their approval, might have run for class president, and might have lost badly, and who might, thereafter, have vowed to take revenge on all those who denied him office—the liberal, the humorous, the nuanced and nonwhite—and who would assiduously plot and plan and conspire, until, finally, he would achieve his revenge by attaching himself to a cretinous sociopath who, like him, was afraid of everything and had never been able to make friends, and would not mind being the executor of this bald, friendless Santa Monican's final redress.

But the searchers were not sure of any of this. These were only private speculations, for they had never seen a man like this, who hid in the nether regions of the ship, whose shape was bent and rigid with loathing, whose skin had never seen light and whose blue-ringed eyes were languorous and dull. The searchers asked who he was, what he was doing there, how long had he been hiding in this vent, but he offered no answer. His mouth moved but no words emerged. He pointed up his vent, as if to say, "Where did he go?" The searchers had no idea what he was talking about, and because he seemed too fragile to move, they left him there, planning to later send food and medical care his way.

Something about the man in the vent brought to the searchers' minds the Captain, and made them wonder where the Captain was, so they continued through the ship, checking every last door and chamber and rounded corner. Among the passengers searching the ship were more than a few supporters of the Captain, and they walked through the black corridors feeling a new sense of dread. There was no sign of the Captain. The wipe-away board had been free of his scrawlings for days.

One of the few remaining officers, who knew the ship and had served under previous captains, had a hunch and looked near the stern of the ship, and confirmed what she and many others suspected. The last remaining lifeboat, a ceremonial sort of craft, with gold accents and built with every luxury, was gone. This last lifeboat had been hidden and never before used, and would have been difficult for the thieves to know about or remove. But it was easy for the Captain to find and use, so he found it and used it.

The Most Foul were surprised and crestfallen for many minutes, finding it hard to believe that a man who had baldly stated, every day of his life, that no one was more important than himself, had in the end put himself above the rest of the passengers. He had led them to great harm and great shame, had ransacked half the ship and had allowed the ransacking of the rest, and had then escaped in a golden lifeboat without a goodbye or thank you or sorry. For the Most Foul, it did not add up.

As for the Kindly Mutineers, they were deeply relieved that the Captain had left on his own, thus freeing them from the conundrum of having to do anything personally to save the *Glory,* themselves, their children, Certain People, and the integrity and honor of all aboard.

"Now what?" said Ava, the orphaned girl who had first warned about electing the Captain to his captaincy, and who had in the intervening months turned thirteen and was so shaken and world-weary that she could not imagine that the adults around her, who had risked so much and who had allowed the suffering of so many, would have any idea what to do now. She did not wait for them to answer.

"First, dignity," she said.

With Ava leading the passengers, they freed those humans still rotting in cages. Some were still alive and might be saved, so they were brought to the infirmary and cared for. Those who had passed away, within sight of the thousands of passengers who did nothing for them, were given a proper burial at sea, befitting a fellow human. When all the people who had suffered under the Captain were cared for and restored to their dignity—as much as was possible after such horror—the passengers looked around and again had no clue what to do.

"Now let's clean," said the grandfather from the beginning of the story. He picked up a mop—the thieves had not been interested in mops—and began mopping. Others swabbed and scrubbed and swept, restoring what they could. Finally, after many days of ablution, the ship looked somewhat like the bright and cheerful place it had been before the ascendance of the Captain and his coterie.

"But we're still adrift," said Ava, who, despite the cleaning and the restoration, still had no faith whatsoever in the adults around her. The passengers searched the bridge and found no navigational equipment, new or old, nothing to salvage and nothing to tell them north from south, east from west. Even the antique sextants and quadrants were gone. And of course they all remembered the many nights when the manuals that explained how the ship was to be steered were ceremoniously thrown from the ship, churned in its mad white wake. And so without engines or rudders, and without the books that told the *Glory* how to be the *Glory,* the ship continued to drift, and the passengers were too tired and too paralyzed to do anything about it. They had forgotten all they knew about the *Glory's* life before.

"Look!" said Ava one day. She pointed to a series of tiny vessels approaching the ship. They were the kind of pitiful rafts and junks and dinghies that the Captain and his Snowmen had blown from the water, had cannoned and sunk. But though the *Glory's* passengers had forgotten just about everything of their history, a precious few of them remembered that at one point they had had compassion for people like this, those approaching by boat with nothing, nothing, nothing, nothing.

And so they lowered ropes and ladders and made ready to welcome those who had drifted to them, while they, too, were drifting. But when the vessels got closer, and the people aboard became clearer, the ship's passengers saw that they were not coming empty-handed. They had no food, and they had little water, but in each of these tiny vessels, there were the distinctive orange-covered books that had once lined the bridge of the *Glory.*

"We found these in the sea," said the first of the boat

people who climbed aboard the *Glory*. This woman was ragged and underfed and tired, but her smile was wide and she was very happy to be aboard the large and sturdy ship, about which she'd heard so much for so long.

She explained that her boat had encountered a few of the orange-clad books hundreds of miles away, and that the steady string of them had led her boat, and others, like breadcrumbs, to the *Glory*. She and the others in her boat knew these books, were familiar with the sober and soaring words within, and knew them to be the words of a noble people who believed in these words, these precepts, more than they believed in the despots and charlatans and strongmen who bent so many other countries to their will and whim.

"We figured you'd want these back," the woman said, and just then a young man arrived—her son—and he had another of the books of the *Glory*. A girl, only seven, followed, and she too carried one of the manuals. She was lifted aboard, and dozens more came aboard from this first woeful vessel and from many more that followed, each of them carrying these books of laws and ideals, and in their presence and in their gifts, the storm-tossed humans looking for a ship in which to survive the seas provided some hope that the *Glory* might know again the meaning of its name.

ACKNOWLEDGMENTS

The author is indebted to Jenny Jackson, Andy Ward, John Gall, Sonny Mehta, Maris Dyer, Rita Madrigal, Nathaniel Russell, John Warner, Em-J Staples, Kitania Folk, John McMurtrie, Peter Ferry, Amanda Uhle, Mark Liebovich, SV, TS, EI and VV.